SAWYER'S SECRET

LAURA SCOTT

CHAPTER ONE

Naomi Palmer shrank into the corner of the back seat of the car, as far away from the leering man beside her as she could manage.

She'd thought following the boxy white van would get her a step closer to finding her sixteen-year-old half sister, Kate, but she hadn't anticipated they'd notice her vehicle behind them and send someone after her. She hadn't been prepared when a car had rear-ended her, sending her spinning out of control.

Since her goal was to find her sister, Naomi had gone along with the leering man without putting up a fight.

A decision she deeply regretted with every passing second and every passing mile. Especially since the white van had disappeared from view around the curvy mountainous road. The Smoky Mountains outside Chattanooga, Tennessee, were beautiful, but she sensed the majestic hills held terrible secrets.

Was her sister being held somewhere in the mountains? Or had she already been moved to a new location?

"Where are you taking me?" Naomi tried to keep her voice steady, but she felt her strength slipping beneath the waves of fear and panic.

What if she couldn't get away? What if they drugged her, or worse?

Kate? Where are you? Are you okay? Or am I already too late?

"You'll find out soon enough." The leering man's guttural voice sent tendrils of dread down her spine. Naomi didn't dare take her eyes from him. The vehicle wasn't going that fast, the curves in the road prevented them from speeding, yet she feared jumping from the car could cause more harm than what these men had planned for her.

A risk she may be forced to take.

Dear Lord, help me! Guide me! Protect me!

"Keep an eye out for the road," the leering man said to the driver. Her pulse spiked as the vehicle slowed as if it was about to make a turn. A quick glance confirmed there was nothing but a dirt road looming up ahead.

They were going to rape and kill her. The thought popped into her head as she understood the magnitude of her foolish actions. It was now or never. As much as she wanted to find Kate, she couldn't let these two men hurt her.

Feeling behind her for the door handle, Naomi took a deep breath, then abruptly lashed out with her foot, catching the unsuspecting leering man beneath his chin with a fierce kick. His head snapped back, hitting the window sharply. At the same moment, she opened the passenger door and rolled out of the moving car.

Years of gymnastics and cheerleading helped her now. Her teeth snapped together as she hit the pavement hard, but she didn't hesitate. Rolling with the momentum of her fall, she quickly leaped to her feet and sprinted as fast as she could in the opposite direction.

The car behind her stopped, and she knew the two men would be hot on her trail. But that didn't worry her as much as being trapped in the car with them.

Naomi headed into the dense woods, using the brush for cover. It was difficult going, but she ignored the scratches from the brambles, her desperate gaze searching for a place to hide.

The two men crashed into the woods behind her. They were large and out of shape, so she felt good about her head start and her ability to lose them. Yet she worried there were more men who could be called in to assist in finding her.

She refused to let that happen.

Leaping over low bushes and using the larger trees for cover helped create a bigger gap from the men behind her. They were swearing and blaming each other for her escape, which made her smile grimly.

When exhaustion finally overwhelmed her, she dropped behind a large tree and took several deep breaths in an attempt to calm her racing heart. She listened intently but didn't hear anything.

Because the men had stopped searching? Or because they'd called in reinforcements and were waiting for them to arrive?

She shivered and took in another deep breath. No sense in borrowing trouble, as her mother liked to say. Naomi would have to take the threats one at a time.

Peering around the tree trunk, she searched for any sign of the men. Darkness was falling fast, which was both a blessing and a curse. When she didn't see anything behind her, she decided to keep going, but quietly this time. She desperately wanted more distance between herself and the leering man.

Her T-shirt was torn, her right shoulder and elbow throbbing painfully from where she'd hit the pavement. She wore running shoes, which weren't as good over the rough terrain as sturdy hiking boots. Still, Naomi pressed forward, moving silently through the woods.

Estimating the time to be about eight thirty in the evening, she figured she had barely thirty minutes of daylight yet, maybe less considering her position beneath the thick canopy of trees. Thankfully, the June temperatures were warm. While she wasn't an avid camper, she took some comfort in knowing she wouldn't freeze to death if she had to spend the night in the woods.

Not that there weren't other dangers. Like more men searching for her. Oh, and wild animals, like mountain lions. And bears.

Gulp.

Naomi moved in what she hoped was a parallel path to the road. She didn't want to meet up with the leering man and his buddy, but she didn't want to get lost in the forest either.

Would they expect her to follow the road? Had they gone back to get the car? Were they out on the road, waiting for her to emerge from the brush?

Naomi wasn't sure what to do other than continue moving through the woods. Time had no meaning, although her surroundings grew darker and darker as the sun dropped below the horizon. When she stumbled across what looked in the darkness to be an actual hiking trail, she hesitated.

Use the trail? Or stay hidden?

Torn with indecision, she glanced up toward the dark sky.

Lord, help me! Guide me!

A sense of peace draped her like a cloak. She glanced back at the trail, noting it headed down the slope of the mountain in the general direction where she believed the road to be located.

Steeling her resolve, she walked along the path, alert to any hint of someone following. She was surrounded by silence, broken only by the occasional hooting of an owl or belching tree frog.

She felt alone in this section of the woods.

For now.

After another ten minutes of hiking, she abruptly stopped when she caught a glimpse of the blacktop mountain road between the trees. Her pulse skyrocketed, and she dropped down along the edge of the trail, intently watching.

The vehicle the men had used to rear-end her was an older model black Buick. But in the darkness, she'd never be able to tell if the car going past on the road was a Buick or something else. She swallowed hard. Naomi wasn't sure how long she crouched there, but when her knees protested the position, she slowly rose and continued easing down the trail. No easy task in the darkness that both shielded her and created a treacherous descent.

When she rounded a curve, the road disappeared from sight. She decided leaving the trail was probably best, to stay hidden from view.

But moving through the brush created more noise than she liked. Again, she was torn by indecision. She took one step forward, then another.

The rumbling sound of an engine made her freeze. It was loud—not a car, she quickly deduced, but maybe a truck. Easing forward to see the stretch of the road better, she watched a pair of high, wide headlights along with several smaller yellow lights along the top roll into view. A semitruck!

Wait for me! Naomi knew her chance to escape this nightmare was driving right past her. She crashed through the brush and ran as fast as she dared down the trail toward the road. But she was too late. By the time she'd gotten halfway there, the truck was no longer in view.

No! She bent over, resting her hands on her knees, trying not to cry. She pulled herself together with an effort. Okay, at least she knew this road saw some traffic other than the men in the black Buick who were no doubt still out there trying to find her.

Naomi continued on the path heading toward the road. Of course, she didn't see any more traffic go by. She told herself to be glad there was no sign of a dark-colored sedan. Upon reaching the bottom of the trail, she paused by a tree located near the side of the road.

Another vehicle was approaching. Not the loud rumble of a semitruck trailer, unfortunately.

Tensing with fear, she eased farther back into the brush, just in case the car was the black Buick. But when she caught a glimpse of a pale car, along with the red and white light rack stretched across the top, she leaped forward, stumbling out onto the road, waving her arms over her head like a maniac.

"I'm here! I'm here!" Naomi wasn't sure why she was yelling those words. It wasn't as if the cop behind the wheel had been out searching for her. "Help me!"

To her overwhelming relief, the squad pulled over to the

side and came to a jarring stop. Tears pricked her eyes as she ran forward.

"Ma'am? Are you all right?" A tall officer with short dark hair slid out from behind the wheel. She noticed he rested his right hand on his gun.

"I-I escaped, two men grabbed me, black Buick—" She stopped, realizing she was babbling. "They rear-ended me, then kidnapped me," she finally managed.

"Do you have a weapon?" The cop eyed her warily as he moved forward. Naomi knew she looked like a crazy woman, her blond hair snarled from the brush and her clothing ripped and torn.

She stared at him blankly, then shook her head. "No."

The name tag beneath his badge identified him as Murphy. He raked his gaze over her. "What about drugs?"

"No!" She was growing impatient now. "I don't have anything because they kidnapped me!"

"Okay, but I need to be sure, for my safety and yours." Officer Murphy stepped closer, finally dropping his hand from his gun. He quickly patted her jean pockets, then glanced over her shoulder. "You escaped and hid in the woods?"

"Yes." Reaction from her ordeal had set in, and she found herself shivering despite the warm temperatures. "I—think they—were going to r-rape and k-kill me."

Officer Murphy's eyes filled with compassion. He rested a reassuring hand on her shoulder. "It's okay, you're safe now."

She gave a jerky nod, still shivering uncontrollably. The cop gently guided her to the squad, opening the front passenger door rather than the rear one, a small gesture she appreciated. "Get inside, I'll keep you safe," he promised.

After sliding into the passenger seat, she rested her head against the cushion and let out a long sigh.

She believed him.

CHATTANOOGA POLICE OFFICER Sawyer Murphy couldn't believe this beautiful girl had managed to escape two men who'd kidnapped her and very likely would have sexually assaulted her.

He'd been working a local case of a young girl's disappearance that he believed was related to human trafficking. He wasn't a detective yet, despite having taken and passed the exam, but that didn't stop him from doing what he could as a patrol officer. Glancing at the slender woman beside him, he realized she might have been taken by the same men who'd grabbed Louisa.

"What's your name?" He started the car and pulled back out onto the mountain road.

"Naomi Palmer." She clutched her hands tightly together in her lap as her body trembled.

"I'm Officer Sawyer Murphy." He glanced at her again, catching her gaze. The darkness made it difficult to see her eyes clearly, but he knew she was still scared to death. "Are you hurt? It might be a good idea for you to be seen at the hospital."

She shook her head. "No need, they didn't get a chance to hurt me."

"But you have a lot of scrapes and scratches," Sawyer gently pointed out. "I'd feel better if a doctor checked you out."

"No doctor." Her tone was firm, and he was glad to see she'd stopped shaking. "The bruises and scratches are because I rolled out of a moving car and tore through the woods."

"You did?" He couldn't help but admire her determination. "I'm surprised you didn't break any bones while doing that stunt."

She shrugged, a glimmer of a smile tugging at the corner of her mouth. "I was a gymnast. I learned at an early age how to tuck and roll."

"I'm impressed." He figured a gymnast would know her body well enough to decide if a doctor was needed. "Can I take you home, Naomi?"

She looked away to stare out the passenger-side window for several long moments before turning back to face him. "Unfortunately, I'm far from home and don't have any money or a phone. My car was damaged and likely has been towed by now. Honestly, I'm not sure what to do."

His heart went out to her. Sawyer knew what it was like to be on your own without a dime in your pocket or anything to eat. Thirteen years ago, when he was fourteen, he'd escaped a horrible foster home run by a man who claimed to be a Preacher but who had physically and emotionally abused him and his foster siblings. When they'd managed to escape the cabin engulfed in a deadly fire, he and the six others who'd gotten out alive had vowed never to go back into the foster system again.

Had Naomi escaped something similar? Her clothes were nothing fancy, yet she had been a gymnast, so she must have lived with a decent family at some point. Sawyer decided to tread carefully, unwilling to add to the trauma she'd already suffered this day.

"I can take you to the police station. After I take your statement, you can use our phone to call someone to help you." He'd been on his way home after a long day, but he wouldn't hesitate to turn around to head back into town.

She shook her head and stared down at her hands. It was difficult to think clearly. "I—can't tell you much about the two men. All I know is they drove a black Buick sedan. And I don't have anyone to call. If I could get to my car . . ." Her voice trailed off.

He glanced at her. "Do you know where it is?"

"No." Naomi's voice was so soft he could barely hear it.

Sawyer sighed and considered his options. As a cop, he knew the best place for her was at the police station. Even though she wasn't under arrest and hadn't done anything wrong, she could spend the night there safely enough.

But he was tempted to bring her to his place. Crazy, since he didn't know anything about her. Maybe it was the fact that she reminded him of Hailey, Darby, Jayme, and Caitlyn, his foster sisters who'd also escaped the fire. There had been seven of them, and he'd encouraged the boys to pair up with the girls, but instead, the girls had drifted off on their own. Jayme, the oldest, had taken Caitlyn, the youngest, under her wing, while Hailey and Darby had gone off together, leaving Sawyer with Cooper and Trent.

Thirteen years, yet somehow looking at Naomi it felt like yesterday.

"A-are you going to take me to jail?"

Naomi's question hit him square in the center of his chest. "No, you're not under arrest, Naomi. I would like to get you someplace safe, though."

She wiped at her eyes and seemed to pull herself together. "Yes, a safe place would be nice."

A horrible thought suddenly hit him. Was she a minor? A runaway? "How old are you?"

"Twenty-six, why?"

He was shocked but tried not to show it. She was only a year younger than he was. "I—you look younger, that's all."

"I've heard that before, but I promise I'm twenty-six." Naomi glanced at him. "I don't want to ask for money, but if I could borrow enough for a motel room, just for what's left of the night, I promise to pay you back."

"I don't mind paying for a motel room, but I don't like the idea of you being alone." He hesitated, then added, "I have a two-bedroom cabin that isn't far from here. If you trust that I won't hurt you, I have a guest room available, free of charge."

"I can't impose," Naomi said. She put a hand to her head. "Besides, I don't really know anything about you. I wish I could remember where my car was. We drove for what seemed like forever."

"If your car was towed, we won't be able to get it until the morning." Sawyer could see she was hesitant to take him up on his offer, and he couldn't blame her. She'd been the victim of a terrible crime. The last thing she'd want was to be alone in a cabin with him. "I grew up in the foster system; you remind me a bit of my younger foster siblings."

She glanced at him in surprise.

"I have a better idea." He pressed on the brake so he could turn around. "We'll get connecting rooms at a local motel. You'll have your own space without being alone."

"No, really, it's fine." She put a hand on his arm, the first time she'd voluntarily touched him. "Your cabin will work, although I don't usually go home with strangers."

"Very smart, and I want you to be sure." He kept the car in reverse. "Downtown Chattanooga is only about twenty miles from here."

"Positive." Her voice was firm. "I very much appreciate your offer, thank you."

It was his turn to hesitate. Sawyer knew he was crossing the line, as a cop he shouldn't bring Naomi anywhere near his home. But he couldn't turn his back on her situation either. And they were only five minutes from his place.

Hoping he wouldn't regret the impulse, he put the squad in gear and continued down the road toward his cabin. Naomi would be safe there, and he'd help her find her car and get money in the morning. It was the least he could do. By helping her, he'd feel as if he were belatedly helping his foster sisters.

Chattanooga wasn't a large city compared to Nashville or Knoxville, but Sawyer preferred living away from others. A holdover from the years he'd spent with the Preacher.

When they weren't being beaten with a switch or forced to kneel and pray for their sins for hours on end, they had been homeschooled by the Preacher's wife, Ruth. And they'd done chores, like cleaning the cabin and caring for the vegetable garden.

Sawyer had enjoyed garden duty and had studied the plants native to the area around Cherokee, North Carolina, with great interest. And he'd eventually used that knowledge to his advantage.

When he realized he was gripping the steering wheel tightly enough to make his knuckles white, he forced himself to relax.

Thirteen years ago, his life had irrevocably changed forever. The horrible fire that had broken out in the Preacher's cabin had nearly killed them all. He and the other foster kids had been forced to sleep in the cellar, and he still wasn't sure how they'd managed to escape.

But the Preacher and his wife, Ruth, had died in the fire that night.

And Sawyer knew that their deaths were his fault.

Because of what he'd done. Guilt still ate at him, even all these years later.

Not that he'd intended the Preacher and Ruth to die. Because he hadn't.

But the end result was undeniable.

To this day, he'd never told anyone what he'd done. It was a secret he'd kept all these years.

One he planned to take to his grave.

CHAPTER TWO

Naomi's mind spun in a dozen different directions. She couldn't quite figure out why she felt safe with Officer Sawyer Murphy. She should be avoiding all men, yet the cop who'd rescued her had been nothing but respectful and considerate of her situation. She hadn't gotten any of the creepy vibes from him that she'd sensed the minute leering man had grabbed her. She even found herself believing his comment about being in the foster system.

Yet she also sensed Officer Murphy had a loner mentality.

His cabin was surprisingly warm and comfortable. Unusually clean and tidy, which made her realize he might have a girlfriend, someone who visited on a regular basis. For all she knew, his girlfriend might even clean for him.

"Are you hungry?" He glanced at her as she sank into a seat at the solid oak kitchen table. "I was planning to throw in a frozen pizza for dinner."

"That would be nice, thanks." Naomi watched as he turned on the oven, then pulled the pizza out of the freezer. "I want to thank you again for bringing me here. I hope you don't get in trouble or anything. I'm sure this isn't exactly standard protocol."

He glanced at her. "No, it's not. But it's the least I can do."

She nodded, her thoughts finally coming together. She probably needed to come clean, to tell him about her younger half sister's disappearance. Now that she was safe, she couldn't be sure the leering man who'd grabbed her after running her into the ditch was the same one involved in Kate's disappearance. There could be more than one man out there interested in grabbing young attractive girls for nefarious purposes.

Officer Murphy would think she's crazy if she tried to explain how she'd followed the boxy white van out of Dalton, Georgia. She'd been run off the road roughly twenty minutes later, just after crossing into Tennessee. She gave herself a mental shake. Why had she bothered following the white van at all? There had to be thousands of white vans driving around the country. Okay, they weren't all boxy in shape, but still.

Except the fact that she'd been rear-ended and grabbed indicated she might have been on the right track. Unless she'd become a target because she looked younger than her actual age.

It was all so confusing. The near miss of being killed, staggering.

"Naomi?" She lifted her head, belatedly realizing Officer Murphy was talking to her.

"I'm sorry, what did you say?" She flushed beneath his dark curious gaze.

"I'm going to change out of my uniform and wanted to know if you'd like to borrow one of my T-shirts. It will be too big, but it's clean."

She glanced down at her torn, bloodstained, and dirty shirt. "That would be nice, thank you."

"I'll be back in a moment. Keep an eye on the pizza." He disappeared down a short hallway, presumably leading to the bedrooms.

She drew a hand through her tangled hair and tried to think of the best way to approach the topic of her missing sister. Maybe tomorrow morning was soon enough. Hadn't he mentioned taking her to the station to take her statement?

Naomi had to believe the men in the black Buick were long gone. If they had intended to kill her and leave her in the woods, there'd be no reason for them to stick around. And for all she knew, the white van had doubled back to head south toward Atlanta, or north toward Nashville.

To give herself something to do other than stew about the mistakes she'd made, Naomi rose and went over to crack the oven door. The pizza wasn't close to being ready.

When she heard a noise behind her, she startled badly, banging into the oven as she spun around. Officer Murphy stood there, wearing casual clothes, jeans and a short-sleeved shirt, holding a dark blue T-shirt in his hand.

"I'm sorry, I didn't mean to scare you." His dark gaze was sympathetic as he held out the shirt. "Bathroom is down the hall to your right. It has a lock on the door, just as the spare bedroom does."

"Thanks." The spurt of adrenaline sent her pulse into double digits. She tried to slow her breathing as she took the offered T-shirt and edged around him to find the bathroom. The way he'd reassured her about the locks made her glad she'd decided to trust him.

After closing the door behind her, she carefully set the clean shirt on the top of the commode. The cotton fabric was soft and carried a hint of Sawyer Murphy's musky scent. She told herself to get a grip and washed at the sink, scrubbing the dirt from her hands and face.

She wasn't looking for a man. Certainly not one who lived so far from her home. It had only been two months since she'd broken things off with Tony Baldwin, her former boyfriend. And truthfully, she hadn't missed him very much. His working night shift at a local carpet factory while she worked days at the outpatient health clinic meant they didn't see each other often.

And when they had been together, they'd often argued.

Tony claimed she was difficult and unrealistic when it came to her expectations about a relationship. And he was probably right. She'd been mildly attracted to him, but the fact that he'd pressed so hard for intimacy had bothered her. He should have respected her desire to wait.

Instead, he'd given her an ultimatum. So she'd walked away.

Obviously, she was better off without him. She stared at her reflection in the mirror, wincing at the mess of her hair. Using her fingers, she tried to comb through the tangles. Her efforts weren't very successful.

Whatever. She wasn't here to win a beauty contest.

When Naomi returned to the kitchen, she found two places had been set at the table. The domesticated scene made her want to smile.

"I have water and a variety of soft drinks." He raised a brow. "Which would you prefer?"

"Water is fine." She was one of those weird creatures that didn't like the taste of most soft drinks. Coffee or water, those were her staples in life.

Officer Murphy filled two glasses with ice water and handed one to her. "Sit down, the pizza will be ready soon."

She sipped her water and resumed her seat. Her stomach rumbled loudly, making her blush. "I haven't eaten in a while."

He eyed her thoughtfully for a moment. "I can always make a second pizza."

"No, this should be fine." How embarrassing.

He pulled the pizza from the oven and set about cutting it into triangles. When that was finished, he set it in the center of the table.

Naomi clasped her hands in her lap and sent up a quick silent prayer thanking God for bringing Officer Murphy to her aid and for the food they were about to eat. When she lifted her head, she noticed Officer Murphy was sitting motionless, waiting for her to finish.

"Thanks again for dinner, Officer Murphy," she said, reaching for another slice.

"You may as well call me Sawyer," he said dryly. "I'm officially off duty."

She nodded but didn't respond as her mouth was already full of the tangy pizza and gooey melted cheese.

"Are you sure you don't have someone you can call?"

She chewed, swallowed, then glanced at him. "I have a friend, Amy, but she's working over the next few days. I'd hate to have her miss work."

"What about family?" Sawyer pressed.

She stared down at her pizza for a long moment, the meal congealing in her stomach. "Would it be okay if we talk about this tomorrow?"

He stared at her as if trying to read what was going through her mind. She couldn't very well call Kate as her half sister was missing. And their mother was gone, having died of cancer six months ago. Her stepfather had left years ago, leaving Naomi solely responsible for Kate's welfare.

No way was she going to call Tony, which left her coworkers at the clinic as the only alternative for help. Coworkers that she wasn't all that close to as she was still relatively new in her clinic nurse role. Amy was the nicest of the bunch, but honestly, they weren't that close. Besides, she'd called in sick for her shifts, something they wouldn't appreciate.

"Sure," Sawyer finally agreed. "Tomorrow morning works fine."

Her appetite had vanished, but she forced herself to eat anyway. Supporting her sister had taught her to take advantage of eating when the opportunity presented itself. Not that they'd gone hungry often, but there had been some difficult times when she'd struggled to make the mortgage payments.

Now her sister was gone and her damaged car was likely towed. Naomi felt as if her entire world was crumbling down upon her. She felt helpless, considering the Dalton police department hadn't done squat to find Kate, emphasizing the fact that there had been no indication of foul play.

Would Sawyer Murphy believe Kate to be a runaway as well? The boxy white van a figment of her imagination?

Or would he believe her?

SAWYER COULD TELL something was bothering Naomi. *More,* he thought, *than narrowly escaping two men who'd kidnapped her.*

But she apparently wasn't ready to confide in him. It went against the grain to sit by and wait until morning, but the beautiful woman seated across from him was so pale, tense, and skittish, he couldn't bear to force the issue. He wanted to help those in need, the way Joe had done for him.

If Joseph Kohl hadn't given Sawyer a helping hand eleven years ago, his own life would have likely turned out very different. After learning he was stealing to eat, the cop who'd arrested him had dropped the charges and brought Sawyer home with him. At the time, Sawyer had considered stealing from the burly cop, then hightailing it out of there. To this day, he wasn't sure what had made him change his mind. Sawyer had stayed, taking the offered food, clothing, and shelter. Amazingly, all had been provided with no strings attached.

Over time, Joe's support had helped him lose the chip on his shoulder and let go of his past. Joe hadn't necessarily said much about God, but one statement had stuck with Sawyer. *Let go of the hate or there will be no room for love.* Sawyer had done his best to honor the cop's wishes, except letting go of the hate he'd harbored toward the Preacher and his wife.

Sawyer wished Cooper and Trent had stayed with him, but within that first rough year after escaping the Preacher, the two boys had taken off, insisting on going their own way. At the time, it had been all Sawyer could do to take care of himself. When Joe had rescued him, and the burly cop had heard his story, Joe had insisted on trying to find his foster brothers. Without success.

Shaking off the morose thought, he focused on the present. When Naomi finished her three slices of pizza, she stood and began clearing the table. "I can do it," he protested, reaching for the last slice.

"It's the least I can do." She avoided his direct gaze, and he found himself wondering if she might disappear in the dead of night. Although, really, where could she go on foot? Chattanooga was twenty miles from here.

He quickly finished the last of the pizza. "Let me show you the guest room," he offered. "I have a spare toothbrush, and you should feel free to borrow anything else you might need."

"Thanks again." She dried her hands on a dishtowel.

The situation was awkward, to say the least. He led the way to the guest room, then disappeared into the bathroom to grab the extra toothbrush and small sample toothpaste he'd recently gotten from the dentist's office.

"Make yourself at home, Naomi." He smiled, then backed out of the room, providing the privacy she deserved.

He waited until she'd finished in the bathroom before taking his turn. Afterward, he crawled into bed and tried to sleep.

Unfortunately, the day's events kept swirling around and around in his head. Starting with Louisa Marchese's disappearance without a trace and ending with stumbling across Naomi Palmer running out of the woods waving her arms at him.

He'd wondered again if the two incidents were related. Louisa's mother claimed her teenage daughter had run off to meet with her boyfriend, leaving a note behind, whereas Naomi had been driving in her car before being run off the road and kidnapped. Two very different scenarios.

Still, they were also both young women involved in something that smelled abhorrently of sex trafficking. Granted, Naomi was older than Louisa by over ten years, but she'd looked young enough to be high school age.

Besides, Sawyer didn't believe in coincidences.

He must have fallen asleep because a creaking noise

had him bolting upright in bed. A glance at the clock on his dresser indicated it was four in the morning.

It took a moment for him to remember he had a houseguest. Moving quietly, he pulled on his jeans and discarded shirt, then grabbed his gun. He crept barefoot from his room.

The door to Naomi's guest room was open, but he didn't see any lights. He continued down the hall, listening intently.

Knowing his house, he was able to avoid the creaking floorboard. The one Naomi had stepped on.

Was it that she was having trouble sleeping? He couldn't blame her, yet her moving around in the dark bothered him. It felt as if she was trying to be sneaky.

Was she going to steal from him? Had she made up the whole kidnapping story?

At the end of the short hallway, he stood, giving his eyes additional time to adjust. He frowned when he didn't see any sign of her.

For a moment he thought she might have decided to take off in his squad, then he remembered he had the keys.

Had she really left on foot?

He crossed the open-living kitchen space to the front window. There were no streetlights out here, and the leafy tree branches along with the always-present mist hovering in the air obliterated most of the light from the moon. Still, there was just enough ambient light for him to see the dark silhouette of a woman, standing several feet from the squad, her arms wrapped around her body as if she were chilled to the bone.

Sawyer let out his breath in a silent whoosh of relief.

She hadn't stolen from him or left on her own.

He stood for a moment, unwilling to scare her by going outside yet unable to leave her alone.

Calling himself all kinds of crazy, he opened the front door and softly called, "Naomi? Are you okay?"

Even though he'd kept his voice hushed, she startled just as badly as she had earlier in the kitchen. He stepped outside, wishing he'd put his shoes on.

"I can take you into town, if you'd rather be around other people," he offered. "Just give me a few minutes to finish getting dressed."

"No, it's fine." Naomi walked toward him. "I'm sorry I woke you."

"Having trouble sleeping?" He stepped back, silently encouraging her to come back inside.

She crossed the threshold and shrugged. "Had a nightmare and couldn't fall back asleep."

"I'm sorry to hear that." He knew all about having nightmares; his escape from the fire in the Preacher's cabin haunted him even all these years later.

Mostly because of the role he'd played in the Preacher's death.

"You didn't cause the nightmare." Her voice was testy, as if she was low on patience.

"Still, I'm sure being in a strange place with a cop you don't know isn't helping." He hesitated, then added, "I've had my share of nightmares, so I understand what you're going through."

She glanced at him in surprise, then nodded. "I thought I heard a car outside."

"Really?" He glanced through the window at his long and winding driveway. "My place isn't visible from the road."

"I know." She shrugged. "Most of the time, fear is irrational."

"And sometimes it's your brain's way of warning you of a dangerous situation," he countered. "In my line of work, I depend a lot on my gut instinct."

"Yes, well, not this time. I didn't see anyone out there." Her tone was light, but he sensed that she'd truly believed she'd been found by the men who'd kidnapped her.

"You want to talk about it?" He padded into the kitchen. "I can make coffee."

"It's pretty early, don't you want to try and get more sleep?" Her protest sounded weak, although he appreciated the effort.

"Nah." He waved a hand and began filling the coffee carafe with water. "At this point, falling back to sleep will be useless."

For long moments neither of them spoke, waiting as the machine finished brewing. When the coffee was ready, he filled two mugs and brought them to the table.

"Milk and sugar?"

"Yes, please." Naomi cradled her hands around the mug as if seeking warmth. Which was strange because the temperature outside was warm and humid. The moisture in the air gave the Smoky Mountains its name.

Years of being on the force had taught him to drink his coffee black, but he watched with amusement as Naomi added a significant amount of milk and sugar to her mug.

She took a sip before meeting his gaze. "I guess I should start at the beginning."

"Okay." He told himself to be prepared for the worst, but Naomi surprised him.

"I live in Dalton, Georgia. My half sister, Kate, lives with me. Well, she did until she went missing two days ago."

"Missing?" He straightened in his seat and leaned forward. "She ran away?"

Naomi shook her head. "I don't think so. I mean, sure, things haven't been great since our mom died, but we've been getting along okay. She got a job at the local carpet factory for the summer."

A sense of dread hit hard. "How old is Kate?"

"Sixteen." Naomi stared for a long moment at her coffee. "I think she was kidnapped, the same way I was."

He waited for her to meet his gaze. "What makes you think that?"

"The boxy white van." She waved a hand. "I know it sounds crazy, but one of Kate's friends, Tamera, said she thought Kate got a ride home from work by a guy driving a box-shaped white van. Only, she never came home."

"Go on," he encouraged.

"I was driving around searching for Kate when I saw a boxy white van just outside of Dalton. I decided to follow it. I was so focused on making sure I didn't lose it while staying far enough back, or so I thought, to avoid being seen, that I never noticed the car coming up behind me. Until it was too late. Next thing I know, my car is flying into the ditch after being rear-ended."

"And where was this crash you mentioned?"

"Just over the Tennessee border, but I was on Highway 71, which I think is the opposite direction from Chattanooga." She frowned. "Right?"

"Yeah, Highway 71 goes straight north from Dalton, while Chattanooga is farther west." He frowned. "Are you sure the ultimate destination was Chattanooga?"

"I'm not sure of anything," Naomi admitted. "I saw a sign indicating we were in Chattanooga, so I assumed so. I know it's silly to follow a boxy white van when there are hundreds of them, but after I was rear-ended and forced off the road, I figured I was onto something. That the white van I was following was likely the same one used to kidnap my sister."

"That would be a huge coincidence," he pointed out slowly. "Yet it's interesting you were rear-ended and kidnapped."

"I hoped they'd take me to where my sister was located," she confessed. "But suddenly I had the feeling they were simply going to get rid of me, dump my body in the woods, so I panicked and escaped."

He couldn't believe she'd basically set herself up as bait. "You took an incredible risk." His tone came out sharper than he intended.

"I know." She lifted her chin, and there was no way to ignore the stubborn glint in her blue eyes. "But I need your help to find Kate. The Dalton police have no leads, and since there's no evidence of foul play, they're not exactly jumping on this as a high priority. They actually told me that Kate likely ran away and would come home when she got hungry. Dalton is normally a boring town. You realize it's known as the carpet capital of the world because of all the manufacturing of flooring done there, right? I mean, it's not Atlanta, or Macon, that's for sure."

He nodded. "Do you have a picture of Kate?"

She grimaced. "In my wallet. I was forced to leave my purse behind when I was kidnapped."

"Does she look like you?" he persisted.

"Similar height and weight. Her hair is darker than mine." She waved a hand. "That doesn't matter at the moment. I have to believe the white van was heading for Chattanooga, Tennessee, for a reason," Naomi said thoughtfully. "Of course, I'm immediately thinking the worst, like it was the next stop in their sex-trafficking operation. And I think they had those men take me out to prevent me from finding the truth."

He stared at her for a long moment. Was Naomi right? Was Chattanooga one of the stops in a sex-trafficking ring?

And if so, was it possible the same sex traffickers had already taken Louisa out of state?

CHAPTER THREE

Naomi felt better having told Sawyer about Kate being missing and what she'd done. In her nightmare, Naomi heard Kate crying out for her sister to save her. Kate had been trapped in the back of the boxy white van, her face pressed against the rear window. Although, in reality, there was no rear window in the van Naomi had followed.

The mere memory of the dream made her shiver. She felt sick at the thought that she may already be too late.

"I'd like you to talk to our detective and work with a sketch artist to create a likeness of the two men who grabbed you." Sawyer's low husky voice broke into her thoughts. "Will you do that for me?"

"Of course." She hesitated, then added, "I'd also like try to find the spot in the road where I escaped."

"I was already planning to take you back to the general area, to see if you could pinpoint the location," Sawyer agreed. His dark brown eyes regarded her thoughtfully. "I'm sure you'd also like to make a few phone calls."

She grimaced and looked away. "I honestly don't know

who I'd call, other than a local towing company to see if they have my car."

"What about your dad?"

"Kate and I share the same mother, but she passed away six months ago from cancer. My dad apparently left when I was just a baby, I never knew the man. Kate's dad stayed a little longer, but he ended up leaving, too, when Kate was five." She shrugged. "My mother didn't have very good taste in men, at least the kind of man who was interested in settling down and having a family."

"I'm sorry to hear that." Sawyer's tone was full of compassion. "I can relate to not having a great family life."

"Really?" For some reason that surprised her. Sawyer seemed so—put together and confident. Not that it was fair to look at him through a stereotypical lens. "I'm Kate's legal guardian because she's only sixteen. A fact she doesn't appreciate, to be honest." She drew in a deep breath. "Still, I'm worried sick something awful has happened to her."

"There's a runaway here in town, Louisa Marchese, who is about the same age as Kate. I'm happy to help as there's a chance these cases are linked, although I don't have any jurisdiction in Dalton, Georgia."

"I know. But if Kate is still here in Chattanooga, then we still have a chance to find her." Naomi didn't want to consider the alternative.

"Maybe the Feds need to be involved," Sawyer mused. "This is potentially a crime being committed across state lines."

She shrugged. "Whatever you think is best. But you should know the Dalton police didn't exactly jump on my theory of Kate being kidnapped for sex trafficking. When they learned about our mother dying and me being appointed Kate's guardian, they immediately went with the theory that she ran away under her own free will."

Sawyer's jaw clenched. "Shouldn't matter why she's missing, at sixteen, she's a minor and vulnerable. Lots of runaways end up getting caught up and forced into sex trafficking."

"I know." She was humbled by Sawyer's outrage on her behalf. "I never imagined something like this could happen to me and Kate."

"I understand." Sawyer reached out to lightly touch her hand, then went to refill their coffee mugs. "I'll make breakfast, although I only have eggs and oatmeal to offer."

She wasn't very hungry but understood that Sawyer needed to eat. "Works for me."

Sawyer smiled and turned to pull out what he needed. Naomi swallowed hard, annoyed with herself for feeling a rush of attraction.

What in the world was wrong with her? How could she think about how handsome Sawyer was while Kate was being held by sex traffickers?

Sawyer was a means to an end. A nice guy and a local cop who'd agreed to help her. She thought about Louisa Marchese, the missing girl he'd mentioned. Were the two girls together? Naomi thought it unlikely, yet two missing girls about the same age within forty-five miles seemed too much of a coincidence too.

"Did Kate talk about having a boyfriend?" Sawyer glanced at her over his shoulder as he cracked eggs into a sizzling frypan.

"No, but that doesn't mean she didn't have one." She grimaced. "Things have been tense between us in the past few months. Kate was fine with living with me after Mom died, until I was granted custody as her guardian. Suddenly she decided she didn't like me telling her what to do, where to go, who to see." She shook her head. "I guess being her big sister was fine, but being her surrogate mother was out of the question."

"I can imagine how hard that was for you both." Sawyer turned his attention back to the stove. "But really, Kate was lucky to have you, Naomi."

"Thanks." Ridiculous tears welled in her eyes. Sawyer was so kind, it made her think about how Tony Baldwin had gotten mad because she wouldn't sleep with him. Squaring her shoulders, she swiped the tears away.

She was through with men. At least for the next couple of years, until she was able to get Kate safely through college.

Her stomach clenched. First, she had to find Kate.

Surprisingly, by the time Sawyer set down a plate of scrambled eggs and a bowl of oatmeal beside her, her stomach was rumbling with hunger. Naomi closed her eyes for a moment and once again silently thanked God for sending Sawyer to her rescue and for the food He'd given her. This time, when she opened her eyes, she found Sawyer looking at her strangely.

She flushed. "Something wrong?"

"No." He hesitated, then added, "I guess you believe in God."

"Yes." She eyed him thoughtfully. "I take it you don't?"

He shrugged and avoided her gaze. "No. I mean, there's so many bad things going on in the world. Hard to imagine why God would allow that to happen."

"My faith has been shaken by Kate's disappearance too," she admitted. She sampled the scrambled eggs. "But whenever I pray, even during times that seem hopeless, I feel God's presence watching over me."

"Maybe because you're innocent in all this," Sawyer said. "Not all of us are."

That seemed an odd statement for him to make, especially as he was a cop. "None of us are innocent, Sawyer. That's why God sent Jesus to die for our sins."

He was silent for a long moment. "Some are less innocent than others."

Was he talking about the sex traffickers? She could understand how difficult it was to believe in God's grace in a world where men preyed on innocent young girls.

"That's true." She thought it might be best to change the subject. "This is great, thank you. I guess I was hungry after all."

"You're welcome." He dug into his own meal, but with slightly less enthusiasm. She felt bad for poking at a sore subject, especially after the way he'd kindly brought her into his home.

"You really think a sketch artist can help?"

He nodded. "They're not perfect, but it's a place to start. And helps us get something out to the other officers on patrol so they can keep their eyes open."

"I'm game to try," she hastened to reassure him. "I didn't get a very good look at the driver, but leering guy was sitting right next to me."

"Leering guy?"

"Well, he didn't introduce himself," she said a bit defensively. "And he leered at me the entire time."

"I'm sorry you had to go through that." Sawyer's tone was gentle.

"It could have been worse." Way worse. She forced a smile. "I'm blessed that you came driving by when you did. Otherwise, I was hoping to flag down a semitruck."

"I'm glad I was there to help." Sawyer finished his eggs and started on his oatmeal.

They ate in silence for several minutes. When she was finished, she took her plate and bowl to the sink. "More coffee?"

"Thanks," Sawyer said with a nod.

She filled his cup, then filled the sink with soapy water. He'd provided the food and cooked for her, the least she could do was wash the dishes.

"You don't have to do that," he protested.

"I insist." She reached over his shoulder to take his dirty plate. "I'm sure you need to shower and change."

He finished his oatmeal and handed her the bowl. "I think we should stop and get you a few items as well."

It was overwhelming to think about how she'd need to get a new driver's license, report her credit and debit cards as stolen, not to mention find out where her car was. Having no cash, cards, or even an ID was a very difficult position to be in.

"I have money in my bank account back home." *Not a lot*, she thought, thrusting her hands into the soapy water, but hopefully enough. "As I said last night, I'll pay you back."

"I'm not worried about that," Sawyer said firmly. "All that matters is that you're safe and that we try to find these guys who kidnapped you."

"I hope we can find them." She continued washing dishes as Sawyer left to use the bathroom.

In her mind's eye, she brought up the image of leering man. She had a very clear image of him but wasn't convinced she'd be able to tell the sketch artist enough to create a decent likeness of the guy.

She'd finished the dishes and was sitting at the table waiting when Sawyer emerged from the hallway. He looked incredibly handsome in his uniform. With her tangled hair, and wearing his oversized T-shirt, she felt like a bum in comparison.

"Bathroom is all yours."

She nodded and slipped past him. It didn't take her long to wash up at the sink. As much as she longed for a shower, without a brush or a comb, her hair would come out looking far worse than it did now.

Besides, it didn't matter what she looked like. The most important thing was to find leering man and his driving buddy.

Sawyer had her sit in the front seat of the squad again, which she was grateful for. Being in the back, behind the cage, would have made her feel like a criminal.

She peered closely at the side of the road, searching for the area she'd sensed the kidnappers were taking her. "There!"

Her shout had Sawyer stepping on the brake, bringing them to a stop. He threw the gearshift into reverse and backed up a bit. "That dirt road?" he asked.

"Yes." Her heart pounded as she realized she'd actually remembered it. "Leering guy told the driver to keep an eye out for the road. We never made it onto the road because I escaped from the car as he was slowing down to take the turn."

"Let's see where it goes." Sawyer's tone was grim as he turned onto the dirt road. Calling it a dirt road was being kind; it was more like a rutted track. The squad bounced up and down as Sawyer eased forward.

The track road ended abruptly. She stared, realizing there was no cabin or any other structure there. Just woods.

"I don't understand," she said in a low voice.

"It's like the road goes nowhere," Sawyer agreed. He glanced at her. "It's a good thing you escaped, Naomi."

"Yes." A wave of dizziness hit as she realized how close she'd come to dying. She shook it off with an effort. "It makes me wonder, though, how those guys knew about this dirt road that basically goes nowhere."

"That's a very good question." Sawyer stared at their surroundings for a moment before throwing the gearshift in reverse again in order to head back to the highway. "We may have to come back later to check the perimeter more closely, see if there's a walking path somewhere nearby."

She reached out to grasp his arm. "Wait, Sawyer, maybe we should do that now?"

"No, I need to do that with other officers, not a civilian. Besides, I really need you to work with the sketch artist."

She bristled at being called a civilian. As Kate's sister, she had a right to search for her. Yet she decided not to argue. As Sawyer drove into Chattanooga, she sent up another silent prayer asking God to watch over Kate.

SAWYER COULDN'T DENY BEING INTRIGUED by the dirt road that led nowhere. From what he could tell, there wasn't a walking path nearby, but he itched to hike the surrounding area just to be sure.

Something he would have done if not for having Naomi in the squad beside him. He couldn't bring himself to place her in more danger. Not to mention, he needed to arrange for backup. And if he found something, he'd have to let Detective Turner, the guy assigned to Louisa's case, know about it too.

The hour was still early, barely 6:00 a.m., by the time

they walked into the Chattanooga police station. The place was never empty, some of the cops working graveyard were making their way in from patrol. A couple eyed Naomi curiously.

"Please have a seat." He pulled out a chair beside his cubicle desk. "It may take a while for me to get the sketch artist in. And I don't think Detective Turner is in yet either."

"It's okay, I can wait." She glanced around, obviously curious. He remembered her saying she'd been a gymnast and imagined she may not have ever been inside a police station before.

"I'd offer you some coffee, but it's not very good."

She shook her head. "I've had more than enough."

Naomi was a bit of an enigma. Unfortunately, his job wasn't to figure out what made her tick but to help her identify the men who'd kidnapped her.

Dropping into his desk chair, he made the call to Dave Campine, the sketch artist, who surprisingly answered despite the early hour. "Dave? I need you to come in to do a sketch as soon as possible."

"Yeah, okay, give me fifteen minutes."

Sawyer glanced at his watch. "Sounds good, thanks."

When that was finished, he placed a call to Turner, but the detective didn't answer. While he waited, he performed a quick computer search on towing companies. He found two that were likely prospects.

"Naomi, what is the make and model of your vehicle?"

"I drive a 2013 blue Toyota Camry."

He typed in the information. "What's the license plate number?"

"Um." She frowned. "I think it's QEP 603. Or maybe the numbers come first."

"Close enough." He picked up the phone and made the calls. The second towing company had her vehicle. "We'll be there later this morning to pick it up," Sawyer told the guy. "Did you find any personal belongings in the vehicle?"

"Nothing," the guy said. "There's minor damage to the rear end, and the frame of the door is bent inward, preventing the car from being driven. Oh, and one of the tires is flat too."

Great. He glanced at Naomi who was listening intently to his side of the conversation. "If you can fix the bent frame and the tire to make it drivable, I'd appreciate it."

"Sure, no problem. Won't take more than an hour."

He replaced the phone and smiled. "Good news, we'll be able to pick up your car very soon."

"But they didn't find my purse?"

"No, sorry." He glanced at his watch again, anxious to get back out to the dirt road to nowhere. "Let's worry about one problem at a time. Getting your car repaired is the first step. From there, we'll figure out the rest."

She sighed and nodded. "I know, I truly am glad they found my car."

He stood and gestured to his chair. "Why don't you sit here and make the calls to your bank and credit card company to report them as stolen? Once Dave gets here to work on the sketch, I'm going to head back out to the dirt road."

"Can't I come with you?" Her blue eyes pleaded with him. "I'd like to be there if you find Kate."

The odds of him finding Kate, or Louisa for that matter, this quickly were a zillion to one. "I'm sorry, but I can't bring you along, Naomi."

"But . . ."

He lifted a hand to stop her. "No. Please trust that I'll let you know the minute we find her."

She grimaced and reluctantly nodded. "I do trust you. I just want to be there for Kate."

"I know. But first we have to find her." *And Louisa,* he thought grimly.

True to his word, Dave arrived to work on the sketch. When Sawyer had Dave and Naomi situated in an interrogation room to work on the drawing, he went to find someone to accompany him back to the dirt road.

"Kevin, do you have time to take a ride with me?" He found Officer Hine kicking back and drinking a cup of super strong coffee.

"Where to?" Kevin set the cup aside and rose to his feet.

Sawyer filled him in on Naomi Palmer's escape from the two men who'd run her off the road, then kidnapped her. "We found a dirt road that leads into the woods, but then just stops dead."

"Probably a place where kids go to make out," Kevin pointed out.

"Okay, but that doesn't explain how the kidnappers knew about it," he argued. "The guy actually said something about looking for the road."

Hine nodded. "Point taken." Kevin Hine settled his hat on his head. "All right, let's check it out."

"Thanks." Sawyer led the way outside to where he'd left his squad. He figured it would take at least an hour for Dave Campine to work with Naomi on the sketch of the guy she referred to as leering man. He and Kevin would hopefully be back by then. And Turner should be in by then too.

Sawyer knew it wasn't likely they'd find anything. Still, he felt the familiar kick of adrenaline as they parked their squads on the dirt road to nowhere and climbed out.

"I'll go left, you take the right," he told Hine. "Radio me if you find something."

"Got it." Hine gamely trudged through the thick undergrowth to the right of the dirt road.

Sawyer did the same, the slight burst of excitement quickly fading. It was clear that no one had come this way in the recent past. There was some evidence of trampled foliage and broken branches, but he knew they could be the result of animals moving through the area. Not necessarily a human.

He scowled. This was likely nothing but a wild goose chase, still he pressed on, knowing he wouldn't be satisfied until he'd cleared the area for himself.

When he stumbled across a path, he followed it, quickening his pace. As he came around a large boulder, he abruptly stopped when he caught a glimpse of a wooden shanty.

It looked like something that might be used as a deer blind by a hunter. He didn't follow his own order to radio Hine about what he'd found. Instead, Sawyer pulled his weapon and edged closer to the shanty, listening intently for any sound that would indicate someone might be inside.

All he heard was the sound of a woodpecker hammering at a nearby tree.

Easing up to the shanty, he kept his back against the rough wooden boards while moving toward the small opening. He was six feet tall, and the opening was right at his eye level, which seemed odd if the shanty belonged to a hunter.

Didn't most hunters sit down to wait for their target to show up?

Holding his breath, Sawyer peered through the opening. The place was empty.

He backed off, then used his radio to get Keven. There

were scuffled footprints on the floor, and there wasn't a chair or other furniture inside.

Sawyer wasn't sure what this place had been used for, but he didn't think it was for hunting. At least, not recently.

Unfortunately, if the runaway girls had been brought here at some point, they were long gone now.

CHAPTER FOUR

Naomi shifted uncomfortably in her seat as the man named Dave Campine began sketching on his pad. He asked dozens of questions about the man's head shape, hair, jaw, eyes, nose, mouth, until she wanted to scream with frustration.

As much as she'd thought she'd gotten a good look at leering man, she was seriously doubting her ability to create a reasonable likeness. Her fault, not Dave's. She was doing her best but feared that this endeavor was a waste of time.

"What about his eyebrows?" Dave eyed her curiously. "Bushy or thin and curved or not very?"

"Bushy and straight." She honestly hadn't paid much attention to leering man's eyebrows. "But he didn't have a unibrow either. There was a gap between his eyebrows."

"Okay, that's good." Dave often gave her encouraging comments even though she suspected he was frustrated with her lack of detail as much as she was.

She wondered what Sawyer had found on the dirt road to nowhere. He'd promised to call if he found Kate, but of course, she hadn't heard a word since she began working with Dave. Sawyer would have to call someone here in the precinct as he didn't have a way to contact her directly.

Not having a cell phone made her feel vulnerable and alone. No way to stay in touch with anyone. Even to get help in replacing her stolen credit and debit cards along with getting access to cash.

Not that she planned on calling her ex, Tony Baldwin. Tony had been a jerk, and she'd made it clear she wanted nothing more to do with him. Although she wouldn't have minded his expertise in fixing cars. Tony was good at all things mechanically related and really could be doing far better for himself than working at the carpet factory.

Not that his career choice or lack thereof was her problem.

"How does this look?"

Dave's question brought her attention back to the issue at hand. When he turned the sketch to show her, she gasped in shock. "That's him."

"You did a great job feeding me details, Naomi." Dave held her gaze. "Is there anything you think I should tweak?"

She stared at leering man's likeness. "His nose was a little bigger and his lips thinner."

"Okay." Dave didn't seem irritated with her changes but erased and redrew the man's features. "Is this better?"

She slowly nodded. "I'm shocked at how much it looks like him."

"Do you want to try doing a sketch of the driver?" Dave asked.

Initially she'd told Sawyer and Dave to focus on leering man as she hadn't gotten a very good look at the driver. But now, she nodded. "It can't hurt. I probably won't have as many details, but we can give it a try."

"Let's do it." Dave carefully pulled the sketch off the

pad and set it aside. Naomi had to tear her gaze away from leering man to focus her brain on remembering as much as she could about the driver.

The work seemed tedious. Or maybe it was just that she was feeling impatient because she had no idea what Sawyer had discovered. Probably nothing, although if that was the case, where was he? Shouldn't he have returned to the precinct by now?

"I'm sorry, I didn't get a good look at his mouth," she said when Dave moved on to sketching the driver's face. "Can we start with his eyes? They were close together and narrow, compared to leering man." She'd glimpsed the driver's eyes several times in the rearview mirror.

"Okay," Dave agreed. He sketched for a few minutes, then asked about the eyebrows.

"Not very bushy and more curved. Again, no unibrow."

Naomi provided as much as she could remember about the driver's nose and mouth, but she could only describe them as normal, nothing unusual about them. By the time Dave turned the sketch toward her, she knew without being told it was far too generic to be much help.

"I'm sorry." She shrugged helplessly. "I was in the back seat and never got a good look at his face."

"It's okay, at least one of the sketches turned out really well," Dave assured her.

Noise from outside the room drew Naomi's attention. Seconds later, the door opened. She was relieved to see Sawyer standing there.

"No sign of the girls," he said, answering the unspoken question in her eyes. "How did the sketches turn out?"

"This is leering man." She pointed to the sketch full of detail. "Unfortunately, I didn't get a good look at the driver."

"This is great, Naomi." Sawyer picked up leering man, nodding at Dave in approval. "Good work."

"Naomi is a wonderful witness." Dave grinned. "And it's not her fault if she didn't get to see the driver's face clearly enough."

"Of course not," Sawyer agreed. "I'll get this sketch distributed to all patrol officers."

Naomi was glad to be of some help, even though she felt certain leering man and the driver were far away from Chattanooga by now.

Unless they were still in the process of moving the girls from one place to the next.

Her stomach clenched as she imagined Kate being taken along with the others.

"Naomi, do you need to use the phone to contact your bank?" Sawyer asked.

"Yes." She rose and followed him from the interview room. "I was able to put a hold on the credit card, but the bank wasn't open."

"Any unusual charges on your card?" Sawyer glanced at her.

"No." At the time she'd been relieved, but now she understood that if leering man had used her card, they'd have more to go on to pinpoint their current location. "I'm hoping the same is true for my debit card."

"If these guys are pros, they're not going to be tripped up by using stolen cards." Sawyer gestured for her to take the seat at his desk. "But there's also the possibility someone else might have picked them up."

She nodded and quickly called the bank. They went ahead and put a hold on her debit card, reassuring her that there had been no activity on the card in the past twenty-four hours. She hung up and turned to Sawyer.

"You didn't find anything around the dirt road?" she asked.

Sawyer hesitated. "I didn't say that; I said there was no sign of any girls. There was a small shanty set up about fifty yards from the dirt road. The place was empty and could have been a deer blind used by hunters. It could be that the shanty isn't being used for anything remotely criminal."

"But if that's the case, how did leering man know the road was there?"

Sawyer nodded. "I've been asking myself the same thing. We've sent a crime scene tech out to see what they can find, but I don't want you to get your hopes up that this will lead to us finding your sister."

She slumped back in the chair, feeling dejected. "So, basically we have nothing."

"We have your sketch, Naomi. And we'll keep working the case. Detective Turner will need to take your statement, but your sketch will help the most."

She straightened and stared at him. "Is this your way of telling me to go home?"

He sighed and rubbed the back of his neck. "There's really nothing more you can do here. In fact, it's probably better for you to be home in case Kate manages to get away from her kidnappers and finds her way back."

There was no denying his idea had merit, but she couldn't just go home and go back to work without doing anything more to find Kate. "I don't think I can leave, Sawyer. Not when I'm the only one who can identify leering man."

His dark eyes held hers for a long moment. "We have your sketch, Naomi. If we find him, we'd certainly let you know."

She looked away, not happy with his response.

"Let's pick up your car, then decide our next steps. I understand how difficult it is for you to leave, but I need you to trust me. I won't stop looking for Kate and Louisa."

She wanted to argue, especially since there was no way to know for sure the two young women were together. But getting her car would be helpful. Not that she had a current driver's license at the moment. Or money.

Maybe Sawyer was right. A trip back to Dalton might help get her back on track. Yet she really didn't want to leave. She'd felt close to Kate here in Chattanooga. As if some force was telling her Kate was nearby.

But for all she knew that sense of closeness was nothing but a figment of her imagination.

"Come on, let's pick up your car." Sawyer stood and held out his hand.

She accepted his hand, keenly aware of the warmth and strength of his fingers around hers.

He escorted her through the precinct. The place was much busier now than it had been earlier this morning. Several uniformed officers were standing around talking and drinking coffee.

A flare of annoyance hit hard. Shouldn't they be out on the streets? Searching for criminals, especially a man with a likeness to her sketch?

"They'll be out on the road shortly," Sawyer said, apparently reading her mind.

She pressed her lips together and followed him out to the squad. Soon they were on the road.

When they passed a drug store, she gazed longingly at it, thinking about how nice it would be to have a hairbrush. Then again, Sawyer wanted her to head home rather than stick around Chattanooga.

Dalton was a little less than forty-five minutes from

Chattanooga. If her car was okay, she could head back home long enough to pack an overnight bag. She could also stop at the bank to get cash.

Sawyer couldn't stop her from staying in Chattanooga for the next few days. After all, she planned to take a leave of absence from work, so they wouldn't expect her to return until late next week.

It would be an unpaid leave, but she didn't care. Nothing was as important as finding Kate.

SAWYER HAD a feeling Naomi wasn't leaving town anytime soon. And while he understood her fear and concern for her sister, there really wasn't anything else she could do to find Kate. And anything she tried would likely interfere in the police investigation.

Naomi's near assault and lucky escape should have scared her enough to run screaming back to Dalton. She might believe God was watching over her, but he wasn't convinced.

Living with the Preacher for five years had made him shy away from anything remotely religious. He'd rather depend on himself, and those working around him, than something he couldn't touch or see.

He didn't begrudge Naomi her faith. Yet he certainly didn't understand it.

The tow truck company was just ahead. He glanced at Naomi, who was staring straight ahead, her mind obviously miles away.

"Naomi?" He pulled into the parking lot of the towing company. "You okay?"

"Fine." She pushed open the passenger-side door and

got out of the car. The summer air was warm, the sun burning away the mist.

The towing company wanted a hundred and fifty bucks to release the car, and another fifty for the bent frame and tire repair. Sawyer gladly paid, although Naomi grimaced at the amount.

"I'll pay you back," she repeated.

"I told you not to worry about it." He didn't mind helping her out. Joe had done so much more for him, he liked the idea of paying it forward.

The car's rear end was definitely crumpled, the trunk stuck shut. "Do the taillights work?" Sawyer glanced at the owner. "If they don't, we'll need those repaired too." Naomi wouldn't make it all the way to Dalton with nonworking taillights.

"They work, and I used clear tape to repair the glass, see?" The tow truck owner showed off his handiwork.

"Good, thanks." Sawyer handed the keys to Naomi. "Check to see how much gas you have. We can always top off your tank if needed."

Without saying a word, she took the keys and slid behind the wheel. Then, without warning, she backed up the car and drove off.

Sawyer sighed, deciding not to mention the fact that she didn't have a driver's license, and glanced at the towing company owner. "Thanks for your help."

The guy shrugged. "That's what I'm here for."

Sawyer returned to his squad and drove back to the precinct. He was oddly upset that Naomi had left without saying goodbye, yet what had he expected? She had thanked him several times for what he'd done. And he knew his telling her to go home hadn't been welcome advice.

He shook off the despondency and focused on the next

steps. He was irritated with Turner, although that was nothing new. The detective seemed a decent enough guy, but he certainly wasn't as assertive as Sawyer would have liked. The trail was already cold, and if they didn't find something soon, he feared they never would. Not that he was supposed to be working the case anyway. He wasn't a detective, at least not yet. But he couldn't do nothing either.

Returning to the dirt road to nowhere and the hunting shanty, he nodded to the crime scene techs working around the shanty. "I'm just going to look around," he called out.

"Let us know if you find anything," one of them answered.

He nodded and walked the area again, painstakingly trying to find any hint of evidence that may have been missed.

The relentless summer sun was only partially obscured by the leafy trees. Sweat trickled down his back, but he ignored it. This road and the shanty were the only clues he had, other than Naomi's sketch.

If this place didn't offer anything to go on, then he wasn't sure what else he could do. The idea of failing to find Louisa and Kate was troubling.

These were only two girls he knew, but what about the others? How many others had been taken away from their homes, their families?

And why would God allow such a thing if He was truly watching over them?

At that moment, a hint of something pink caught his eye. He blinked and dropped to his haunches. Gently pushing the foliage out of the way, he saw the small round pink elastic hair band.

A thread of excitement ran through him. Logically, he knew the hair band could have been left by anyone, not necessarily from a girl who'd been targeted by sex traffickers. But its location here, within a stone's throw of the shanty and the dirt road to nowhere seemed too much of a coincidence.

He pulled an evidence bag from his pocket and carefully picked up the hair band. He didn't see any hair strands caught in the elastic, but there was always the possibility that the crime scene techs could find something using a microscope. Getting DNA from this could blow the case wide open.

If they could get it turned around in a reasonable time. Which wasn't likely, given that he had no proof that it belonged to one of the missing girls.

For a second, he wondered how on earth he'd even found the elastic band. He'd been thinking about God when he'd noticed it.

Another coincidence? He gave himself a mental shake. Whatever. It didn't matter how he'd found it. Far more important to get clues from it, if possible.

Buoyed by his find, he continued searching. But after another hour passed, he gave up.

Better to get the pink elastic hair band to the lab than to keep searching the woods. Yet, he headed up to the shanty to see what, if anything, had been found.

The crime scene techs were packing up. "Find anything useful?"

"A partial print off the door handle," the tech answered. "But interestingly enough, no other prints. Almost as if the place had been wiped clean."

"That is strange." Sawyer looked around the shanty curiously. "No reason for a hunter to do that."

"Unless they wear gloves or are poaching," the tech pointed out.

"This close to the road?" Possible, but Sawyer didn't think so. He pulled out the evidence bag and handed it over. "I found this about twenty yards from here. May be nothing, but I'd appreciate you checking for hair follicles that might provide DNA."

"I can do that." The tech put the bag in his pocket. "I'll call you when we get the fingerprint sent through the system too."

"Thanks." Encouraged by the two clues, Sawyer headed back down to the dirt road where he'd left his squad. He found himself wishing he had a way to contact Naomi so he could fill her in on what they'd found and ask if Kate may have been wearing a pink elastic hair band.

He already knew Louisa hadn't been wearing one, at least according to her mother. In the photo he'd been given, Louisa had long dark curly hair that she wore down around her shoulders.

What he needed was a photograph of Kate. He should have asked Naomi to get one from their home in Dalton. He never should have let her drive off without giving her his business card.

Lack of sleep wasn't a good excuse for his mental lapse. He'd gone without sleep plenty of times.

Especially those terrifying days of surviving in the woods after escaping the fire.

Sawyer pushed away the memories of his past. There was nothing he could do to change what he'd done. His role in the Preacher's death was irrefutable. And he wasn't sure why it was bothering him so much these past few weeks.

Well, partially because he'd heard from Hailey Donovan, one of his foster sisters and the one he'd always been closest to. Hailey was currently living in Gatlinburg but was planning to come and see him next week, if they could coordinate their schedules.

He was truly looking forward to connecting with Hailey and shared her desire to find the rest of their foster siblings. But he could do without reliving the horrible memories, thank you very much.

His stomach rumbled with hunger. It was past noon, and he'd eaten breakfast at four thirty in the morning. Sawyer decided to swing by a local family restaurant to eat and radioed the dispatch center so they'd know he was on a meal break.

"Ten-four," the dispatcher replied. "By the way, that woman you had in here earlier, Naomi Palmer? She called looking for you."

"She did?" His heart should not have kicked into triple digits at the news. He pulled into the parking lot of the restaurant and shut down the squad. He cleared his throat. "Do you have a number I can use to call her back?"

"Yeah, let me know when you're ready."

He pulled out his cell phone. "Go."

As the dispatcher read off the numbers, he punched them into his phone. The area code wasn't local, and he wondered if she'd gotten a replacement cell phone for the one she'd lost or if this was a disposable phone.

"Thanks." Sawyer disconnected from the radio and immediately called Naomi. His spirits plummeted when she didn't answer, and there was no voicemail set up for him to leave a message.

The tiny hairs on the back of his neck rose in alarm. What if something bad happened to Naomi?

What if he'd made the wrong decision in sending her home?

CHAPTER FIVE

Naomi had returned home to Dalton, Georgia, just long enough to shower, change, pack a bag, and withdraw cash from the bank. At first they gave her a hard time because of her lack of ID, but thankfully she knew the mortgage department well after dealing with them in taking over her mother's small house after her death, so they gave her what she needed.

She'd purchased a cheap cell phone and considered calling Sawyer. Then scoffed at herself for being foolish. Instead, she hit the road to head back to Chattanooga.

For some strange reason, she'd felt compelled to take the less direct route to Tennessee, heading up Highway 71. The same general area where she'd been rear-ended and kidnapped while following a white van.

As she neared the area where the crash had happened, she'd found herself clutching the steering wheel tightly in a deathlike grip. But then she was past the area and crossing the border.

Highway 71 turned into Highway 60, so she angled west toward Chattanooga. She stopped at a gas station in

East Ridge and nearly had a heart attack when she saw a black Buick parked next to one of the pumps.

The kidnappers?

Naomi's heart pounded so fast she feared it would burst from the center of her chest. Scrunching down in the seat as much as possible, she slowly passed the Buick, memorizing the license plate. Being low in the seat made it difficult to see if there was damage along the front of the Buick. With trembling fingers, she called the Chattanooga police station to ask for Sawyer.

Some friendly lady told her he was out on a call but that she'd give him the message, reassuring her that he'd return her call as soon as possible. Naomi hadn't been happy but gave the number of her newly purchased cell phone. She'd driven past the gas station, afraid to stay too close. What if they were the kidnappers and they noticed the damaged rear end of her car? She shivered despite the warm sun beating through the windows.

No, she couldn't let them see her. But she didn't want them to get away either. If they were in fact the kidnappers.

The car had been empty, the men must have been inside the gas station convenience store, paying for gas and getting something to eat.

Naomi realized she needed to go back, to see if she could catch a glimpse of the owner of the black Buick. Taking several deep breaths in an attempt to slow her racing heart, she looped around the block and approached the gas station again.

There! Someone was getting inside the black Buick!

From the back she couldn't tell if the guy sliding behind the wheel was the same one who'd driven her and leering man away from the scene of her accident.

As the guy pulled away from the gas station, she

followed, keeping a wary eye on her nearly empty gas tank. She edged as close as she dared, her stomach tied in knots. There was only one man in the car, which made her doubt in the fact that the driver was indeed the same guy she'd escaped from.

But she needed to know for sure.

The black Buick headed onto a two-lane exit leading to Interstate 75. Gathering every ounce of courage she possessed, she pressed the gas until she was alongside the Buick. The driver glanced at her, and she stared at him as long as she dared.

Was it the same man? As she hadn't gotten a good look at him the first time, she couldn't be absolutely sure.

But he might know her. A wave of panic had her stomping hard on the brakes, causing several drivers behind her to hit their horns, which had the opposite reaction by drawing more unwanted attention.

Hide! Hide! Naomi frantically looked for a place to get off the highway. Her instincts were screaming at her to put as much distance between herself and the Buick as possible.

She managed to jerk the wheel to get into the next lane, then she hit the gas again to zoom ahead of the car beside her so she could get off on the exit. In some corner of her mind, she heard her cell phone buzzing, but she was too scared to take her hands off the wheel to answer it.

More horns blared, and she found herself ducking down lower in her seat, so much so that she could barely see over the top of the steering wheel. When she reached the bottom of the exit ramp, she instinctively turned west to head into downtown Chattanooga.

Fifteen agonizing minutes later, she pulled into another gas station, her fingers trembling so badly she had trouble picking up the phone. She wanted to believe the driver of the Buick had been the same man who'd kidnapped her, but she knew she couldn't swear to it. And there had been no sign of leering man, which was strange.

Was she losing her mind? Was the guy behind the wheel of the Buick really the same one who'd kidnapped her? He resembled her sketch, but the shape of his mouth and his nose hadn't looked at all familiar.

She rested her forehead against the steering wheel for a long moment, pulling herself together with an effort. When her phone rang again, she managed to pull it from her pocket and answer it.

"Hello?" Even to her own ears, her voice sounded strained.

"Naomi? Are you okay?" Sawyer's voice was panicked, and she belatedly realized he must have been the one who'd called earlier.

"I—think so." She swallowed hard. "Thanks for calling me back."

"Where are you? Are you safe?" His voice softened a bit as he added, "I've been worried sick about you."

"I'm fine." *Sort of.* "I'm outside of East Ridge and have the license plate of a black Buick for you to check out."

There was a brief moment of silence before Sawyer said, "I can do that, but you know there are lots of black Buick vehicles on the road."

"I know. There was only one man in the car, and when I came up alongside him to get a good look at his face, he did resemble my sketch of the driver."

"You what?" Sawyer's voice rose in agitation.

"I had to know, Sawyer." She tried to downplay the danger, even though she'd been scared out of her skin. "Not that it helped, since I never got a good look at the driver during the kidnapping."

Another pause. "What are you doing in East Ridge?"

"Getting gas. Listen, can I give you the license plate information? If it turns out to be nothing, then fine. But it can't hurt to check."

She heard him sigh. "Okay, give it to me."

"Purple, yellow, orange 238."

"Got it. I'll see what we can find out. In the meantime, I have a question for you."

"What?"

"Did Kate wear elastic hair bands?"

Her heart stuttered in her chest. "Yes. Why? Did you find something?"

"Any particular color?" Sawyer asked.

"Her favorite color is blue." She gripped the phone so tightly her fingers ached. "Did you find a blue elastic band?"

"No, sorry. I found a pink one, about twenty yards from the hunter shanty."

She cast back in her memory. "I think Kate has worn a pink one in the past."

"Well, it could be nothing, so don't get your hopes up," he warned. "I have the crime scene techs taking a look at it more closely, see if we can find any hair follicles caught in the elastic. But again, it could be nothing. People hike in the woods all the time. Anyone could have dropped the band."

Logically, she knew he was right, but she couldn't bear to let go of the possibility that Kate had recently been in Chattanooga. "Thanks for telling me, Sawyer. I appreciate it."

"I assume the fact that you're currently in East Ridge means you're not planning to return to Dalton anytime soon."

For the first time in what seemed like forever, the corner

of her mouth tipped up in a smile. "You assume correctly. I'll be back in Chattanooga soon, although I honestly don't know how far away I am."

"Fifteen minutes, tops. Listen, why don't you meet me at the City Café Diner for lunch? It's right off the main highway."

She was pleasantly surprised by his offer. "Okay, see you soon."

Somehow, just talking to Sawyer calmed her nerves. On one hand, she felt certain he'd prefer she return home to Dalton, yet on the other hand, she was glad to be seeing him again when she didn't look like something dragged up from the bottom of the Tennessee River.

———

WHILE WAITING FOR NAOMI, Sawyer used his computer in the squad to run the license plate of the black Buick. The owner was a guy named Melvin Curtis. As he peered at Melvin's driver's license photo, he noted there was only a passing resemblance to Naomi's sketch of the driver.

Interesting that she hadn't been able to recognize him either.

Sawyer put Melvin's name and date of birth into the system, hoping he had some sort of criminal record. The guy had done time for auto theft, but that had been fifteen years ago, when he was twenty-five. Now he was forty, and Sawyer couldn't help but wonder how the guy had gone from auto theft to sex trafficking.

If Melvin was guilty of anything at all.

He glanced up as Naomi pulled in and parked beside him. He quickly pushed out of the squad to join her.

She looked amazing, and still far younger than her twenty-six years. Her blond hair was shiny and clean as it framed her face. She'd changed into clean clothes, nothing fancy. A soft pink T-shirt and blue jeans that hugged her figure. She also must have gotten a replacement phone too.

He had to give her credit for pulling herself together the way she had, despite her horrific ordeal.

"You look great," he said by way of greeting.

"Thanks, although that only makes me think I must have looked awful before," she said wryly.

"Not true." *Idiot.* He mentally kicked himself for making her think that.

"Well, thanks." She blushed and turned toward the entrance to the diner.

Despite being quarter past one o'clock in the afternoon, the place was crowded, likely the result of the summer tourist season. He only saw one empty table and quickly snatched it up.

"Did you run the license plate number for the Buick?" Naomi asked.

"Yes, the guy who owns the vehicle is Melvin Curtis." He watched for any sign of recognition, but she only stared blankly. "Sound familiar?"

"No." She sat back against the seat when their server arrived to bring menus and water.

After placing their orders, she leaned forward again and asked in a low voice, "Can I see the elastic hair band?"

"No, I've already given it to the crime lab." He eyed her steadily. "Try not to get too excited about a simple elastic band. Do you know how many people hike the Smoky Mountains each year?"

She sighed and sat back in her seat. "I know you're

right. It's just . . ." She glanced away. "I can't stand not knowing where Kate is and if she's okay."

"I know." He hesitated, then added, "You should have stayed in Dalton, Naomi. There isn't anything more you can do here."

A spark of anger lit up her blue eyes. "I found a black Buick, which could be the same one used to kidnap me."

Could have been, but not likely. "Melvin doesn't have much of a criminal record. A car theft when he was twenty-five, and that's it. No solicitation for prostitution charges or anything similar. No crimes involving weapons."

Naomi looked dejected at the news. "You don't think he's the same man who'd helped kidnap me."

Sawyer's heart went out to her. He understood her need to make sense out of a situation that was anything but logical. "We're working the case, Naomi. Trust that we'll do our job, okay?"

She stared down at the table for a long moment. "I know you will. But I want to help."

Her helping was only likely to slow them down. He tried another tactic. "What is Kate going to think if she goes home to an empty house?"

She met his gaze. "I left her a note with my new cell number, so hopefully she'll call me."

"If she can get access to a phone," he felt compelled to point out. "If she manages to escape the way you did, she probably won't have a phone or money either."

Her eyes clouded as she frowned. "I hadn't thought of that."

Their server brought their respective meals, and they ate in silence for a bit. He was so relieved Naomi was unhurt that his appetite had returned with a vengeance. He made quick work of his buffalo chicken sandwich and fries.

Naomi picked at her salad, which made him feel bad that he'd ruined her lunch. He smiled reassuringly. "Hey, you can go back to Dalton and be there for Kate when she gets home."

When, not if.

She shook her head. "I'm not going back, Sawyer. I can't. Not yet. I'm the only person who can identify the kidnappers."

Except she hadn't been able to identify the driver, a fact he decided not to reiterate.

When they finished eating, he signaled for the bill. Naomi pulled out some cash, but he waved her away. "I asked you to meet me here, so it's my treat."

"I owe you for the towing and the repairs to my car," she protested. She shoved a couple of hundred-dollar bills toward him. "Take it. Paying you back is the least I can do."

He didn't touch the cash. "Please keep your money, at least for now. There will be plenty of time to square up when this is over."

She stared at him for a long moment. "Would you do this for anyone else?"

He didn't hesitate. "Yes, I would. I promise I only want to help you through this. No strings attached. I, uh, once had a guy do something similar for me." Sawyer normally didn't talk about himself like this, but he wanted to reassure her. "Joe was a cop, too, and helped me out of a jam. I learned to accept his help, the way you should accept mine. I wouldn't be here today if not for him."

"I'm glad to hear you had someone helping you," she said softly. She drew in a deep breath. "Okay, I'll keep the money for now, but I need you to know that I expect to pay my own way."

"I do," he assured her. "Even though I really wish you'd go home."

"You can wish all you want, but I'm staying." She slid out of the booth.

He inwardly sighed and briefly considered arresting her for driving without a license. But doing something like that would only add to her already stressful ordeal.

Although her ability to get a motel room without a credit card and ID would be slim to none. Which may actually force her to head home. He relaxed a bit as he slid out of the booth and followed her outside.

Should he offer his place again? It wasn't as if he was using his guest room.

As soon as the idea flashed in his mind, he thrust it aside. No, what he needed to do was make Naomi realize that her being in Chattanooga was unnecessary. If she couldn't find a motel room, she'd likely head back to Dalton.

Maybe. Hopefully.

"Thanks for lunch, Sawyer." Outside the café, Naomi gave him a solemn look. "Will you please call me if you find something related to my kidnapping or the missing girls?"

"Naomi . . ." He sighed. "I can't talk to you about an ongoing investigation. As I said before, I need you to trust me. Trust the process."

She looked down at the ground and reluctantly nodded. "I'll try." She lifted her gaze. "But you need to understand that I won't rest until I know what happened to Kate. And if that means bothering you every single day, too bad. I don't care. She's only sixteen."

Her defiant gaze made him want to smile. Frankly, he'd be surprised if she only bothered him once a day. "Got it."

She turned to reach for her car door, then stopped and swung back. "Sawyer?"

"Yeah?" He'd opened his own car door and rested his arms along the top.

"I—would you be willing to give me your personal cell phone number?"

He hesitated, knowing it was a bad idea.

"I promise I won't bother you too much," she went on. "But if I see the leering man or the driver of the black Buick, I'd like to be able to call you directly."

Even though it went against protocol, he nodded. After all, by now they were hardly strangers. "Fine. Actually, you already have it. I used my personal cell to call you back. But understand if you become a nuisance, I'll block you." The minute the words left his mouth, he felt foolish. No way would he block Naomi's number.

A fact that bothered him.

"I know, thanks." She pulled out her prepaid phone and stared at the screen. "Is this your number?" She held up the display.

"Yes." She hit the call button, and his phone vibrated in his pocket. "See?" He pulled it out and added her name to the number in his contact list. "We're all set."

"Thanks." She smiled and slid the phone back into her pocket.

"Take care of yourself, Naomi." He had to force himself to slide in behind the wheel. Why on earth was he so attracted to her? Because she was beautiful and strong and had managed to outsmart her kidnappers long enough to escape?

It wasn't as if he didn't serve alongside a couple of capable female officers who were just as brave, because he did. Granted, cops like him took on the risk by donning their uniform each day.

Unlike Naomi who didn't deserve to be in harm's way. It wasn't something she was trained to do.

Although now that he thought about it, he'd never asked about her career. Did she work at one of the carpet factories too? She'd mentioned Kate working there but hadn't said anything about her own role in the community.

Not that it should matter to him one way or the other. Naomi Palmer had been a vulnerable victim in a terrible crime. A victim he refused to take advantage of.

He glanced over, waiting for her to back out of her parking spot first. She gave him a little wave, then slowly rolled her Toyota backward.

Crack!

The gunshot and the resulting shattering glass spurred him into action. He shut off the squad and rolled out of the vehicle, weapon in hand. Keeping his head down, he spoke into the radio on his collar. "Shots fired, repeat, shots fired outside the City Café on Edgerton Road."

Naomi's car was half in and out of the parking spot. Had she been hit? His heart lodged in his throat as he darted around the front of his car, still keeping his head down, to reach her driver's side door.

"Naomi? Are you okay?" He cranked on the door handle, but it was locked.

"Naomi?" He glanced around, then used his baton to crack the rear passenger window open, fearful of raining glass on her. "Are you hit?"

She didn't answer.

CHAPTER SIX

Somewhere off in the distance, beyond the pounding in her head, Naomi heard someone calling her name. A sense of urgency hovered out of reach.

She needed to move, to get away, but her body felt sluggish. If only her head would stop hurting!

"Naomi?" The voice was louder now, so she did her best to focus on the sound. "Unlock your door!"

Realizing she was behind the wheel of a car helped her remember. A loud banging noise and then a window shattering.

With a wince, she lifted her head and tried to look around. Her vision was blurry. Fumbling for the door, she unlocked the car, then lifted a hand to her head.

Her fingers were wet and sticky with blood, and she could feel a gash along the right side of her temple.

No wonder her head hurt.

"Naomi, can you move?" Sawyer had opened her door and was kneeling beside her.

"Yes." She managed to swing her legs out of the car. "I'm okay."

"You don't look okay." Sawyer's tone was grim. "But there's an ambulance on the way."

"It's just a headache." A whopper of one, but nothing she couldn't deal with.

"Stay down." Sawyer helped her out of the car so that she was crouched beside him. "We're going to get into the squad, okay?"

She couldn't nod without lightning bolts of sizzling pain shooting through her head, so she simply followed his lead.

Within seconds, they were safe between the squad and the building. Sawyer was still talking into his radio as wailing sirens filled the air.

Loud. It was all too loud. She covered her ears, wincing as she accidentally hit the wound on her temple.

"Help will be here soon." Sawyer's tone was encouraging. "Hang in there a little longer."

Did she have a choice? It wasn't as if she could go anywhere.

"I need to examine your injury." Sawyer's voice was low and husky. She glanced down at her top and realized her favorite pink T-shirt was covered in blood.

"My bag is in the back of my car." She grasped his arm. "Please get it for me."

"I will as soon as our backup arrives." He looked at something over her head and nodded. "And here they are."

Seconds later, the area outside the restaurant was crawling with cops. It was heartening to know she was safe, but the constant questions were difficult.

"I didn't see anything," she said for what seemed like the tenth time. "I was backing up when I heard the sharp sound and my window shattering. That's it. I didn't even realize I was hit right away. I wish I could tell you more."

"I didn't see anything either," Sawyer said, his voice full

of disgust. "All I can say is that the gunfire came from directly behind us. I think it may have been from a handgun, although I can't swear to it. I was taken by surprise, we don't often hear gunfire in the middle of town."

"We have officers canvassing the area." The man standing next to them appeared to be the guy in charge. "Ma'am? The ambulance is here."

"Okay, but I think the injury looks worse than it is. Head wounds tend to bleed a lot." She knew, based on the pounding in her head, she probably had a concussion too. Too bad. No way was she going to be stuck in a hospital.

The EMTs crowded around her, wiping the worst of the blood away with wet gauze so they could examine her head.

"Looks like she was grazed by the bullet," one of them said to Sawyer.

"I'm well aware of what happened," she said, irrationally annoyed with the way they were talking to Sawyer rather than her. She was the patient after all.

"We need to take her to the hospital," the second EMT said. "They'll want to do a scan of her head."

"I'm right here," she said again. "And I get to decide if I'll go to the hospital or not."

"Naomi, please get checked out." Sawyer looked upset. "You could have a serious head injury."

"I doubt I'd be talking to you if that was the case." Naomi was a nurse, although after her mother had passed away, she'd traded in her critical care nursing job for a lower paying role working in the clinic. The job was more routine, but the hours were better for keeping an eye on Kate. "There isn't much they do for concussions other than rest and make sure the symptoms don't get worse."

"I'd rather hear that from the experts," Sawyer said firmly.

"I'm a nurse, Sawyer." It occurred to her she hadn't told him that before. Not that he'd asked. "I'll agree to get a CT scan, but that's it. I'm not spending the night in the hospital."

The EMTs looked at each other, then shrugged. The first one said, "All we need to do is transport you to the hospital. From there you're on your own."

"Fine." She didn't want to know how much this would cost her. Her mother's medical bills had taken a huge chunk of her savings, which is why her financial situation was somewhat tenuous.

"Thanks. Please take her to Memorial. Naomi? I'll meet you there with your bag," Sawyer promised.

She didn't say anything as the EMTs dressed her wound, then brought over the stretcher. Feeling foolish, she climbed onto the cart and allowed them to transport her to the hospital.

Having never ridden in an ambulance before, she couldn't say she enjoyed it. The ride was rougher than she expected, the sudden movements of the driver making her head hurt worse.

The emergency department seemed busy, but they took her back into a room right away. Considering treatments for concussions involved rest and quiet, the place was anything but.

Naomi didn't see Sawyer again until she'd been poked, prodded, and scanned. When he finally came into her room with her hastily packed gym bag over his shoulder, she grasped his arm. "Please take me home."

"Easy now, we're just waiting for the results of your head scan." Sawyer gazed down at her. "You look better."

Probably because they'd cleaned up most of the blood. Except for what stained her shirt and jeans. "Tell them to hurry and read it. The noise level here is awful."

"Okay, sit tight." He set her gym bag on the chair, then closed the door to her room. The noise level dropped a decibel, making her sigh in relief.

It wasn't until that moment that the reality of the situation sank in. Someone had taken a shot at her car in an attempt to kill her.

Reaching up to lightly touch the bandage over her wound, she grimaced. Had nearly succeeded in killing her. If the bullet had hit even a fraction of an inch to the left, she'd be dead.

Who had done this? Leering man and his sidekick driver? Why? Because she'd escaped? If so, how had they known where to find her?

Recognizing her damaged car wouldn't be that difficult, but that didn't explain how they'd found her at the café. Chattanooga wasn't that small.

She abruptly sat up, then had to grab the side rail to keep from passing out as a wave of pain hit hard. She took several deep breaths in an attempt to ignore it.

Had the driver of the Buick managed to follow her off the interstate? The thought was terrifying.

Although if that was true, then certainly Melvin Curtis was involved in this and could be brought in for questioning.

Naomi gently eased back down against the pillows and closed her eyes.

Note to self: Do not make sudden jerky movements.

She had no idea how long she rested when the door to her room opened, revealing Sawyer and the female physician.

"Your head scan came back negative for a bleed," Dr. Rawlings said. "But you really should stay at least twenty-four hours for observation."

"I'm a former ICU nurse," Naomi informed her. "I know all too well that patients don't get as much peace and quiet as they need while in the hospital. I'd rather be released so I can really rest. I promise to come back if my symptoms change for the worse."

Dr. Rawlings eyed her thoughtfully. "Okay, I trust your judgment. I'll send through the discharge paperwork. A nurse will be in soon."

"Thanks." She tried to smile, but it felt like a grimace.

"You're welcome." Dr. Rawlings patted her arm before turning to leave.

"A critical care nurse," Sawyer repeated with a bemused expression. "You never told me. Very impressive."

"I'm just a clinic nurse now," she said wearily. "Better hours for Kate, no weekends."

"Still, I'm in awe of your talent."

"It's nothing, really." His comment made her wonder what he'd thought she did for work, but she decided he'd assumed she worked in one of the flooring companies. After all, she had mentioned living in the carpet capital of the world. He'd also assumed she was younger than she actually was. "I'd like to change into clean clothes."

Sawyer put down the side rail and helped her sit up. The room spun for a moment, then thankfully righted. A step in the right direction. She eased onto her feet and slowly bent to unzip the gym bag.

She hadn't packed many clothes, but thankfully she had an extra pair of jeans and several shirts. She pulled out something to wear and shuffled into the bathroom.

When she looked at her blood-matted hair along the

right side of her head in the mirror, she sighed. Of course, she once again looked like an escapee from a horror flick. It seemed Sawyer was destined to see her at her worst.

After washing up in the sink and changing into clean clothes, she felt slightly better. When she emerged from the bathroom, her nurse, Lila, was waiting.

"Dr. Rawlings would like you to change the dressing twice a day and to follow up in a week, or sooner if your symptoms get worse."

"I understand, thanks." Naomi took the discharge paperwork, barely glancing at it. She knew the drill better than most.

Sawyer led the way outside where the bright glare of the sun made her wince. He opened the door for her, and she slid into the squad.

Traveling in a police car was beginning to feel routine.

"Can you find me a cheap hotel?" She glanced at Sawyer as he pulled out of the hospital parking lot.

"I'm taking you back to my place," he said. "For one thing, a hotel is going to want to see an ID and credit card, both of which you don't have. And for another, I'm worried about you staying in a hotel all alone. I'd rather be close by to keep an eye on you."

"I'm not going to ignore my health." His lack of trust stung. "You noticed the doc didn't argue when I mentioned the lack of peace and quiet in the hospital. Patients are always better off recuperating at home."

He sighed. "I know, it's just—that was a close call, Naomi. You could have died."

"I know. And I think you should look at that Melvin Curtis guy. He's the only one who could have followed me to the café."

Sawyer's mouth thinned. "Yes, I know. We've issued a BOLO for him and the black Buick."

The news was reassuring. With the entire Chattanooga police department searching for Melvin, she felt certain he'd be arrested and willing to give them information about where the girls were being held.

Dear Lord, please watch over Kate until the police are able to rescue her!

SAWYER GLANCED AT NAOMI, relieved she appeared to be resting. The gash marring her temple could have been so much worse.

He almost thanked God for saving her, but then he gave himself a mental shake. She was the believer, not him. He was fairly certain she was more than willing and able to pray for herself and Kate.

Sawyer was glad his boss hadn't minded his taking the rest of the day off. He'd given his statement before heading over to the hospital, and every moment away from Naomi felt like tiny knives piercing his skin.

He hadn't been able to relax until he'd seen for himself that she was fine. Learning her brain scan was normal had been an even bigger relief.

As he drove to his cabin, he kept his eye out for any sign of the black Buick. It irked him that he hadn't taken Naomi's concern over seeing the kidnapper seriously.

Although even if he had, he wouldn't have expected the guy to shoot at her.

He'd left instructions for her car to be taken to the police station to be searched for evidence, like hopefully the bullet, and when that was finished, he'd arrange for it to be taken to the closest garage. Naomi couldn't drive it until the rear window was repaired.

At the rate these guys were coming after her, she'd need a replacement vehicle before this was over.

He frowned as he slowed down to pull into his driveway, taking care not to jostle the car too much. Turner had promised to question Naomi about her kidnapping but hadn't bothered to ask for a meeting. And the incident at the café bothered him. Why had they taken a shot at her? He also didn't understand why the kidnappers had stayed in Chattanooga when they could have just as easily moved on in search of their next victim.

Unless Naomi had gotten too close when she'd followed the black Buick. Still, he figured they could easily dump the Buick and get another car.

Shooting at Naomi seemed almost—*personal*. As if the kidnappers were carrying out a vendetta against her. Because she'd escaped? Maybe.

Yet Sawyer felt certain there had to be more to it than that. Again, why hadn't they just moved on?

Nothing about this made sense.

Naomi let out a low moan and opened her eyes. "You need a smoother driveway."

He winced. "Sorry about that."

She lifted her hand. "I'm kidding. Thanks for doing this. Although I wish you'd go back to work. I'm sure I'll be fine alone."

"My shift is just about over anyway. And I'll check in later, see if they've picked up Melvin Curtis."

"Okay." Her easy acquiescence proved she wasn't feeling well. Normally he'd expect an argument.

The sooner she was able to get some rest, the better.

He parked the squad and grabbed Naomi's bag from the

back seat. She moved gingerly, and he hoped that wasn't an indication that she was feeling worse.

"You okay?" He unlocked the door and swept a gaze over the interior, before stepping aside to let her in.

"Yes." She entered his home and crossed over to the sofa. She smiled wryly. "I don't suppose you have any acetaminophen?"

"I do." He set the bag down beside her and hurried into the bathroom. He brought out the over-the-counter meds along with a glass of water. "Here you go."

"Thanks." She downed the pills and handed the empty glass and bottle back. "I'm sure I'll feel better soon."

"Go lie down in the guest room," he suggested. "I'll make something light for dinner."

"You don't have to wait on me." She pushed to her feet. "I hate that I'm making more work for you."

"It's no more additional work, I'd make something for myself anyway." He picked up her bag and followed her into the guest room. "Please get some rest and let me know if you need anything."

"Thanks, Sawyer." She gingerly sat on the edge of the bed. He set her bag down, then left her alone, softly closing the door behind him.

He changed out of his uniform but kept his gun on his hip, partially because he felt naked without it, but more so because he knew the danger surrounding Naomi was far from over.

These guys had taken a shot at her with a police cruiser nearby. A bold attempt, and one that didn't bode well. It meant these guys were more worried about getting rid of Naomi than getting caught.

A part of him wished he could patrol the city, doing his

part to find the black Buick. But there was no way he was leaving Naomi here alone.

Determined to check the exterior of his cabin, Sawyer eased out the front door and moved quietly around the structure. His large vegetable and herb garden ran along the entire west side of his home. The front and the back had large clearings, but the east side was full of trees and other foliage.

That would be the most logical place for someone trying to creep up to the cabin to hide. He went back inside for fishing wire so he could set up several low trip wires. Cameras would be better, but he didn't have time to set them up, so he was forced to improvise.

When that task was finished, he spent some time pulling weeds from his garden, a never-ending task. Then he gathered carrots, radishes, and green onions for the chicken soup he was planning to make.

He carried his bounty inside and double locked the front and back doors. Many people didn't bother locking up in this neck of the woods. Especially if they were isolated and away from town. Criminals didn't bother to come out into the woods to find people to rob.

East Ridge, where Naomi had spotted the black Buick, had a surprisingly high crime rate, but in his experience, most of that crime centered around robberies, drugs, and some gang-related events.

But now he wondered if maybe the sex traffickers had made that part of the city a hub for their business.

When he'd finished chopping the vegetables and precooking the chicken, he placed the large pot of soup on the stove to cook. Then he pulled out his laptop and reviewed the area where Louisa had last been seen.

Louisa and her mother didn't live in East Ridge, but

their home wasn't that far from the area either. The kidnappers could easily expand their search area throughout Chattanooga without being far from their home base in East Ridge.

If that was where their home base was located.

He sat back in his chair, staring at the computer. Theories weren't facts, but he very badly wanted to check out the East Ridge gas station where Naomi had seen the Buick.

Maybe later, when she was feeling better.

His cell phone rang, and he recognized his boss's number. "Lieutenant."

"Murphy, I just got a call from the state troopers. They found a purse lying at the side of the road."

He straightened in his seat. "Naomi's?"

"Yeah, her driver's license and credit cards were still inside, but no cash."

"Where did they find it?"

"It was found near the Tennessee-Georgia border, off Highway 60," Lieutenant Evan Watkins said. "Which is exactly where your witness claims the car crash took place."

Sawyer blew out a frustrated breath. Naomi would be glad to have her driver's license back, but the location of the lost purse wasn't helpful.

The only clue they had was Melvin Curtis. And for all they knew, the guy could be in another state by now.

CHAPTER SEVEN

Naomi woke feeling disoriented. Her headache was still there, although slightly less intense than earlier. It took a moment for her to remember where she was.

Sawyer's cabin.

She'd never met a nicer, kinder guy. Or rather, the nice guys she knew weren't nearly as good-looking. The ones who had the looks tended to know it and acted accordingly.

Like her ex, Tony. Who was very attractive and knew it. He'd acted as if she should be glad he was interested in her.

Jerk.

She eased from the bed and made her way to the bathroom. The enticing scent of chicken soup filled the cabin. It was amazing to her that Sawyer knew how to make soup, although for all she knew, he could have run into town to buy it.

Nah, she didn't think that was likely. Partially because Sawyer seemed determined to remain glued to her side. And also because last night, when she'd gone outside after her nightmare, she'd gotten a glimpse of his large vegetable garden. Seeing that had surprised her, she didn't know many men who did their own gardening. At the time she'd wondered if he had a live-in girlfriend.

But she hadn't found any women's toiletries in his bathroom, which convinced her that Sawyer lived alone. At least most of the time.

Naomi washed up in the bathroom, then came out into the kitchen. She wished that she'd packed a large suitcase of clean clothes. She was going through shirts and jeans like toilet paper.

She found Sawyer working on his laptop at the kitchen table. "Hi."

"Hey." His warm smile made her feel a bit dizzy. "Are you feeling better?"

"Yes." She crossed over to peer into the large pot on the stove. "You made chicken soup?"

"Yep. Figured that would be better for you than something heavy."

She replaced the lid and joined him at the table. "Very impressive that you know how to cook."

"Not that impressive since I like to eat." He grinned. "And I don't like wasting veggies from the garden."

He was unlike any man she'd met, although the past year had been one in which she hadn't socialized much. Especially after she'd kicked Tony to the curb. "I noticed your garden. I assume the high chicken wire fence is designed to keep the animals out?"

"The deer are the worst," he said wryly. "And they can jump the fence. I use some natural deer repellant, along with planting various herbs and ferns around the garden that deer and rabbits tend not to like."

"Wow, sounds like having a garden is a lot of work."

He shrugged. "Maybe, but it's worth it."

"Did your foster parents teach you how to garden?"

His expression turned guarded. "The foster home I lived in for five years was an awful place. But yes, I did learn about gardening there, mostly because I used the garden as an opportunity to escape. I would have spent all day there if I could."

"That sounds rough." She felt bad for what he'd been through.

"Yeah." He quickly changed the subject. "Are you hungry? The soup is ready anytime."

"Surprisingly, I am." Initially she'd felt sick to her stomach, a side effect she knew of the concussion.

"I'll get it." Sawyer shut his laptop and crossed to the stove. He ladled soup into two large bowls and carried them to the table. "By the way, I have some good news."

Her heart leaped. "You found Melvin Curtis?"

"No, sorry. Your purse was found at the side of the highway just over the Georgia-Tennessee border. You'll get your driver's license back tomorrow, along with your credit cards."

Since she'd already canceled the cards, that wasn't much help. "I'll be glad to have my driver's license. I don't suppose my cash was still inside?"

"No." Sawyer set what looked to be homemade bread on the table. "How much did you have?"

"Less than a hundred dollars." She tried not to be disappointed. "I'm sure leering man and his driver took it."

"Or some person who found the purse had helped themselves," he added. "At least you have one less thing to worry about with getting your driver's license back."

"Yes." She sampled the soup. "This is really good."

"Thanks."

"Did you make the bread too?"

"Yep. It's not hard with a bread maker." He looked a bit

uncomfortable talking about his prowess in the kitchen. "And as I said, I like to eat."

"Me too, but I've never made bread or grown my own veggies."

"I know what it's like to go hungry. I enjoy cooking."

Her heart squeezed at the thought of a young Sawyer going hungry. What kind of foster family made their children go hungry? "I'm so sorry."

"I'm fine." His curt response indicated he didn't want to discuss the issue any further.

She glanced outside. "I'd like to drive around a bit, check out the city."

"Not tonight." He leveled her a stern glance. "You promised to rest, Naomi."

"Riding in a car isn't exactly stressful," she protested.

"That's not your plan, and you know it. We've issued a BOLO for Melvin Curtis and the black Buick with the license plate number you provided to us. Along with the sketch of your kidnapper. We will find them."

She grimaced. Sitting and doing nothing while Kate was out there, somewhere, wasn't easy. The lack of activity in her current clinic role, compared to being a critical care nurse, had been the most difficult thing to get used to. The hours at the clinic were shorter, and they were busy, but with mundane tasks such as refilling meds and taking calls for patients who wanted to see their doctor. The shorter workday had actually seemed longer than her twelve-hour shifts in the ICU.

Truthfully, she'd keenly missed the hustle and bustle of critical care. Of knowing that patients lived because of her expertise.

She'd never mentioned her dissatisfaction with her new

job to Kate, though. Even when the teenager had started rebelling against her guardianship in a big way.

Maybe someday, when Kate headed off to college, Naomi would return to the career she'd loved.

If they were able to find her sister. Her stomach clenched, and she stared down at her soup.

Not if but when they found Kate. Naomi needed to keep thinking positive.

She couldn't bear to consider the alternative.

SAWYER HAD BEEN ALONE for so long that sharing meals and his living space with Naomi provided a level of intimacy he wasn't prepared for.

He admired her for so many reasons. The way she'd courageously escaped her kidnappers, for being a critical care nurse, and caring so much about her half sister, Kate. Then there was also the fact that Naomi was beautiful without seeming to realize it.

Having feelings for her wasn't smart, and logically, he knew he couldn't act upon them. She was a victim and a witness, which made her off-limits. Plus, Naomi didn't live in Chattanooga and would return to her life in Dalton, Georgia, very soon. Tomorrow, if he had his way.

He was much better off alone.

Especially considering what he'd done thirteen years ago.

"Sawyer?"

Naomi's voice brought him back from his dark thoughts. He met her gaze, belatedly realizing his soup was getting cold. "Yeah?"

"I trust you, or I wouldn't be here. But I'm also not used

to sitting around doing nothing. I really want to help find Kate."

"I know." He honestly couldn't blame her. He knew what it was like to have your family missing.

While she'd been sleeping, he'd decided to pick up his on-again, off-again search for the rest of his foster siblings. It was something he did when he had extra time on his hands, which admittedly wasn't often. Hailey was planning to visit next week, but so far, she was the only sibling he'd connected with. And even then, they didn't get a chance to talk as frequently as he'd have liked.

It shamed him that he hadn't done more to find the others. As a cop, he should have searched for them night and day. Especially knowing Cooper and Trent had gone off on their own.

The biggest factor, though, was the lack of having a last name for his siblings. He'd learned Hailey's was Donovan, but he didn't know the last names of the others. Which probably seemed odd, but when they were with the Preacher, it was all they could do to survive.

Discussing their last names hadn't been high on the list of priorities. And even if he had known their last names, without any formal paperwork like birth certificates and social security numbers, it was as if they didn't exist.

If Joe Kohl hadn't helped Sawyer get his paperwork straightened out, he would never be where he was today. And the faint memory of living in Charleston, North Carolina, had helped in that regard. Sawyer had been nine years old when he'd been sent to the Preacher, so he'd retained some memories of the places he'd lived.

Unfortunately, he wasn't sure if Cooper and Trent, who were both a year younger, could say the same.

For all he knew, they could have obtained fake identities. And if so, his chances of finding them were slim to none.

Reconnecting with Hailey over a couple of phone calls had been enough to spur him into trying again.

"You'll let me come with you tomorrow?"

Huh? Once again, he'd gotten lost in his own thoughts. What had Naomi asked? "I'll bring you with me to the police station so you can get your driver's license, and we can check on your car." And maybe Turner would finally talk to her, although he wasn't going to hold his breath. The guy worked at what seemed to Sawyer to be slower than a snail's pace. "From there, I'd really like you to head home."

She held his gaze for a long moment. He caught a glimpse of disappointment in her eyes before she turned away.

"Okay." She finished her meal without saying anything more.

Sawyer knew she wasn't happy with him, but what could he do? No way could he allow her to go on patrol with him. He'd lose his job if his boss ever found out. Having her stay with him was risky enough.

And taking off work wasn't an option either. Finding Kate and Louisa meant he needed to be out there, following up on any and all possible leads.

Like returning to East Ridge.

"One thing you can do for me is show me the gas station where you saw the black Buick. Maybe we can swing by there before heading to the precinct in the morning."

Naomi looked up in surprise. "Okay. I know exactly where it is."

"Good. The other thing I need you to do is rest. A head injury is nothing to fool around with."

"I'm aware." She reached up to finger the gauze over her

injury. "Makes me realize I should have been more compassionate to my patients in the ICU who had head injuries."

"I'm sure you treated them very well."

The corner of her mouth tipped up in a half smile. "I really loved my job. It wasn't easy, but it also was never boring."

"Is that your way of saying the clinic job is boring?"

She flushed and shrugged. "It's okay. Caring for patients in any setting is important."

"But it's not as interesting as working critical care."

"Not to me. I guess I do miss the adrenaline rush that comes with taking care of the sickest of the sick. I was also a member of our medical emergency response team. It was my job to run out to take care of any patient suffering an abrupt turn for worse."

"I give you a lot of credit for being able to do that," he said honestly.

"Really?" She looked surprised. "You put yourself in danger every day. That's far more important than what I do."

"Not more important, but similar I guess." He finished his soup, stood, and reached for her empty bowl. "I don't often think of it as being in constant danger. My main concern every day is to keep the public safe."

There was a long silence before she said, "Sawyer, may I ask you a question?"

He turned and instinctively tensed but nodded. "Sure."

"Is my being here going to get you into trouble? Either with a girlfriend or at work?"

Hesitating, he shrugged. "No girlfriend, but work? I can't lie, your being here isn't ideal since you're the witness to a crime. I'd rather not tell my boss, if that's what you're asking."

"I'm fine with going to a hotel."

"I'd rather you head home, but we can discuss next steps in the morning."

She stared at him for several heartbeats. "Okay. I guess that's why you can't take me on patrol with you. Honestly, Sawyer, I don't want you to get into trouble over me."

"I won't." It wasn't entirely true. Sawyer knew he was in deep trouble over her. Personally more than professionally.

He cared about Naomi, far too much.

And his feelings toward her, along with her staying with him, could be a big problem if she had to testify at trial against her kidnappers. Which was why he should have insisted on the hotel room.

But he hadn't. And right now he was more concerned with keeping her safe while making sure she didn't suffer a relapse from her head injury than about a nonexistent trial.

Hopefully, this all wouldn't come back to bite him in the rear end.

"I'll get some sleep, then. Thanks for dinner." Naomi was looking a bit peaked again, as if this much activity had been too much for her.

Which only convinced him she had no business driving around town looking for her kidnappers.

Or for Kate.

He washed the dishes, giving Naomi time to use the bathroom. Their early start to the day made it seem later than it was, but Sawyer knew the smart thing to do was to rest when you had the chance.

Sawyer decided to head outside to make another sweep around his cabin before heading to bed. The likelihood of anyone finding them there was slim to none. However, he wasn't about to take any chances.

Not with Naomi's life.

He avoided his fishing line trip wires and was relieved when he didn't find anything out of the ordinary.

The area surrounding his cabin was peaceful and quiet, the way he liked it.

Despite his exhaustion, Sawyer found it difficult to fall asleep. He'd been surprised and secretly pleased that Naomi had asked about his having a girlfriend. It made him think he should have asked about her having a boyfriend, but somehow, he sensed she didn't.

When he dragged his mind off that topic, the shooting outside the café played through his head.

Why on earth would someone take a shot at her when he was in his squad next to her? It seemed like a ridiculous risk to take.

Had the officers canvassing the area come up with anything useful? He considered calling in to find out but figured his boss would have let him know if they'd found something major.

Especially if they'd brought in Melvin Curtis.

A strange thudding sound woke him from a sound sleep. Not the creaking of a floorboard this time, but a muffled sound.

Something tripping and falling in the woods?

One of the kidnappers? Or a wild animal? Sawyer quickly slipped out of bed, taking several precious moments to slide his feet into shoes and to grab his gun and his phone. Naomi's door was closed, so he silently moved through the interior of his living space, avoiding the creaking spot on the floor.

Easing from the cabin and silently locking the door behind him, Sawyer stood outside for a few seconds, allowing his vision to adjust to the darkness.

His heart was pounding, but every sense was on alert.

Years of living in the woods after escaping the fire helped him now. He moved silently, using trees for cover, toward the area where he'd strung the trip wires.

Another rustling sound followed by a whispered curse. Knowing the thudding sound had been made by a person rather than an animal had his pulse skyrocketing.

How had the kidnappers found Naomi here?

He tightened his grip on his phone and briefly considered calling for backup. He rejected the idea for two reasons. He lived so far out of town the intruder would be long gone before anyone had a chance to arrive. And he didn't want to give away his position.

At the moment, he still had the upper hand. The intruder wouldn't have cursed if he'd known Sawyer was out there.

Moving farther into the woods, Sawyer peered through the night in an attempt to find the guy. But the intruder must have realized he'd made too much noise and had stopped moving.

Being on the run and surviving in the wild had taught Sawyer to be patient. He went still and listened.

Was it his imagination? Or had he heard the sound of breathing?

He continued to wait. One minute. Five. Ten.

Had he imagined the intruder? He didn't think so, but anything was possible.

Fifteen minutes, then twenty minutes passed before he heard the intruder moving through the brush. The sounds were faint, indicating the guy was taking his time, stepping carefully to avoid being tripped up again.

Fighting the urge to follow blindly, Sawyer remained still, straining with the effort to pinpoint the intruder's location. He desperately wanted to catch this guy, but he knew the intruder was likely armed.

Especially if he was the same guy who'd taken the shot at Naomi. In that moment, he realized the gunman must have gotten the license plate of his squad. Although, still, his address wasn't available on any public listing.

His thoughts were interrupted when he caught a glimpse of movement to his right.

There! A large dark shape was moving in a direction away from his cabin.

Sawyer silently stepped forward, hoping to close the gap between them. But the intruder must have sensed his presence behind him because a small light came on, and the man began to run.

No! Sawyer quickly followed the man's bouncing light, determined not to let him get away. Then the man abruptly doused his light at the same moment he disappeared behind a large tree.

Sawyer instinctively hit the ground as the echo of a gunshot rang out.

This had to be the same man who'd tried to kill Naomi outside the café.

Sawyer crouched behind some thick brush, again trying to pinpoint the man's location. Without the light, his eyes took a long moment to readjust to the darkness.

The sound of a person crashing through the brush had him leaping to his feet. Running after an armed man was foolish, but Sawyer didn't care.

He could not let this guy get away!

Another gunshot rang out. Sawyer easily imagined the guy simply shooting off his gun over his shoulder as he ran in an effort to keep Sawyer at bay.

The shot hadn't come anywhere close, so Sawyer kept

going. But he was moving slower than the intruder, and suddenly he heard the sound of a car engine.

The Buick? Sawyer put on a burst of speed but was seconds too late. As he came out of the woods, he stared in horror at the red taillights disappearing around the curve.

The armed intruder had gotten away.

CHAPTER EIGHT

Naomi woke to a loud popping noise. For a moment, she was disoriented. Had the sounds been from a dream? Had she relived those moments of being shot in her car?

For several seconds she heard nothing but the sound of her own breathing. She did her best to relax.

Easing out of bed, she quickly dressed. Thankfully, her lingering headache was less intense, making it easy to ignore as she slipped from the guest room.

The door to Sawyer's bedroom was open, as was the bathroom. Fear congealed in her gut as she tiptoed through the cabin. There was no sign of Sawyer, which frightened her more than anything else.

He wouldn't leave her alone without a good reason.

After pulling a knife from the butcher block on the counter, she crossed over to the large picture window overlooking the woods. A quick glance at the front door confirmed it was locked. When she saw a flash of light, her pulse kicked into high gear.

Was Sawyer in trouble? Had the gunman found them?

Reminding herself that Sawyer was an armed cop didn't

help much. There had been two kidnappers, and while she'd seen only the driver in the Buick, the leering guy could have been somewhere else close by.

Like holding the girls, Kate and Louisa, captive.

The light in the woods grew brighter, and moments later, she saw Sawyer emerge from the thicket. Her shoulders slumped in relief to find him unharmed.

He wore a grim expression on his face as he came up to the cabin. She moved away from the window to unlock the door so he could come inside.

"What happened?"

He frowned upon seeing the large butcher knife in her hand. "You should know that most intruders would be able to easily overpower you to get the knife and wouldn't hesitate to use it against you."

"Thanks for the cheery thought." She hated feeling foolish. "What happened out there?"

"I'm fine, nothing to worry about."

"That wasn't my question. Something sent you outside with your gun." She crossed over and replaced the knife in the butcher block.

When she faced him, he looked uncertain, as if deciding how much to tell her.

"Sawyer, please, I deserve to know what happened."

He blew out a breath. "I heard noises outside and chased a man through the woods. He shot at me twice and unfortunately managed to get away."

Panic hit hard. "Are you hurt?"

"He missed," Sawyer said in a reassuring tone. "But I'm trying to understand how he found us here in the first place. It's not like my property is easy to find. You can't see the cabin from the road."

A shiver rippled down her spine. It was a good point. "It's my fault."

"No, it's not." Sawyer's tone was firm. "My squad was parked right next to your Toyota when the shot was fired. He could have gotten my license plate number and followed us. I didn't see anyone following, but maybe with a pair of binoculars he was able to follow us to the general location."

Her knees went weak, and she sank into a kitchen chair. "That only confirms it really is my fault. That he came here for me."

"Try not to think like that." Sawyer came toward her, setting his gun on the table. "You're the victim, Naomi. Those guys kidnapped you. It's not like you asked for this."

She squeezed her eyes shut for a moment. "But I did."

"What do you mean?"

"I voluntarily followed the boxy white van." She opened her eyes and forced herself to meet his gaze. "And when the two men rear-ended me, I didn't try to escape right away. I was hoping they'd take me to wherever they had Kate. Don't you see? I pretty much asked for this."

"No, you didn't." His low husky voice washed over her. He drew her to her feet. "Following a white van isn't a crime. Being rear-ended and kidnapped is. And those men would likely have done worse."

His hand was warm and strong around hers. She clung to it as if it were a lifeline. "I know, but I hate how you're in danger now too."

"Oh, Naomi." He sighed and drew her closer. She didn't resist. "I'm a cop, and as you pointed out earlier, we're always in danger."

"Sawyer." She whispered his name, resting her forehead against his chest. Stunned to realize how much she'd come to care for him in such a short period of time.

Then he was gathering her close, hugging her tightly. She welcomed his embrace, soaking up his warmth and strength like a dry sponge.

Breathing in his musky scent, she secretly longed for Sawyer to kiss her, which was crazy since she barely knew him.

Although she was forced to admit that Sawyer had already proven himself to be more honorable than Tony. By a mile.

The sound of a car engine had Sawyer pulling away. She tightened her grip in an effort to hold on to him. "What if he's come back?"

"No, I'm pretty sure this is the squad I requested for backup." Sawyer smiled reassuringly. "The bad part about living way out in the woods is that the local police aren't readily available."

"Okay." Feeling foolish, she released him. It never occurred to her that he'd called for backup. Sawyer seemed like such a loner, but of course, he worked with other officers in the Chattanooga police department.

"Stay inside," Sawyer said before heading out.

She crossed her arms across her chest, watching through the window as Sawyer met with the officer. The two men spoke briefly before heading over to the woods. Sawyer pointed at something near the ground.

Footprints? She could only hope they found something to lead them to leering guy and/or the driver.

The interior of the cabin was dark. She yawned and debated whether or not to make a pot of coffee. It was three in the morning, and she felt sure Sawyer would want to get more sleep. She had no idea how long he'd been up and out in the woods while she'd been out like a light.

When Sawyer came back inside, he didn't look very happy. "What's wrong?" she asked.

He shook his head. "Other than me seeing the guy and hearing the gunfire, there's no solid evidence the intruder was out there."

"I heard the gunfire too." She frowned. "Why didn't the officer talk to me?"

Sawyer grimaced. "Because I didn't tell him you were staying here. I didn't want to open that can of worms. Besides, even your statement agreeing with what happened here doesn't mean much if there's no hard evidence to prove it."

"Oh." She was embarrassed to realize he'd hidden her presence in the cabin from the officer on duty. Good thing she hadn't gone outside to help. "I thought you were in the woods checking on footprints."

"We were, but we didn't find anything. Not surprising since the woods are really dense. Even though there's a lot of humidity in the air, the ground didn't reveal anything useful."

"Maybe you'll pick up something in the daylight?"

"Possibly. But it doesn't matter. The officer will write a report, which will help if there's an additional attempt." He smiled when she yawned again. "It's still the middle of the night, why don't you get some more sleep?"

She blinked and eyed him thoughtfully. "Are you going to get some sleep too?"

He glanced around the interior of the cabin, rubbing the back of his neck. "I figured I'd stretch out on the sofa for a bit."

Somehow, she knew that meant he wouldn't be getting any more sleep. Her headache was a dull throb, and sleep was critical to her feeling better.

Especially if she was going to leave here to get a hotel room later that morning.

"Okay, good night, Sawyer."

"Good night, Naomi." The way he said her name sent a wave of warmth through her entire body.

Upon returning to the guest room, she had to remind herself that staying with Sawyer was temporary. He wasn't interested in her as a woman but as the victim of a crime. He was searching for the local missing girl along with her half sister.

But as she drifted off to sleep, she imagined being held in his arms and reveling in his kiss.

SAWYER STAYED on the living room sofa. He lightly dozed, waking frequently to assess for potential threats, the way he used to do when he was living and hiding in the woods.

He didn't think it likely that the intruder would return. But old habits never died, and he refused to be caught unaware a second time.

Good thing his trip wires had worked. Sawyer hated to imagine how close the intruder might have gotten if he hadn't put them in place.

He fully intended for Naomi to head home later that morning, but now he wondered if that was the best plan. She lived alone in Dalton, and he had to believe the kidnappers had taken note of her address on her driver's license.

Although they hadn't taken it with them, which was interesting. If he was a bad guy who wanted to track a victim down, he would have kept her driver's license.

Had Naomi's kidnapping been a crime of opportunity?

Maybe.

When the sun brightened the sky, he gave up trying to get any more rest. What he needed was a plan for the day. Naomi would want to get her purse and driver's license, but what about after that? He had to be to the station by seven thirty and didn't like the idea of leaving Naomi alone and vulnerable.

With a head injury no less.

A motel in town might be the best option. If he could get her into a place without being seen. But having her in town would be helpful. While being out on patrol, he could swing by and check on her.

He set about making coffee and breakfast, keeping an eye on the clock. He wasn't sure how much time she'd need to get ready.

But he needn't have worried because he heard Naomi's door open followed by the bathroom door closing before the coffee pot had finished brewing.

Naomi came into the kitchen ten minutes later. "Good morning, Sawyer. I'd ask how you slept, but I'm fairly certain you didn't."

He smiled wryly. "I managed to get some sleep, thanks. Sit down, breakfast will be ready soon. I have to work today, so we need to leave here by seven."

"Okay." She brushed past him to help herself to coffee. "Do you think my car will be repaired before the end of the day?"

"I hope so, but we'll check on their progress." Personally, he cared more about getting the bullet from her vehicle than the repair itself.

They needed something to go on to find these guys. The only good thing about the intruder showing up last night was that it proved the kidnappers were still in the area.

If he were the praying type, he'd ask for God's help in finding and arresting these guys by the end of the day. Before they took off for parts unknown where they might never be found.

He focused on the scrambled eggs in the large frypan. He filled two plates and carried them to the table. "Here you go."

"Thanks, Sawyer." He dropped into the chair across from her and bowed his head, knowing she was going to pray before eating.

"Lord, we thank You for keeping us safe in Your care last night, and we ask that You continue to protect us as we search for Kate. Amen."

Amen. His brain automatically echoed her sentiment, which surprised him. He hadn't stepped foot in a church or prayed since leaving the Preacher. He had a faint memory of attending church with the first foster family he'd lived with back in Charleston. Yet he couldn't shake the Preacher's ranting and raving at them, hitting them while screaming they were going to hell.

So why was he thinking about God now?

Naomi was messing with his head in more ways than one. Not only did he find it incredibly hard not to kiss her last night, but now he was beginning to think more about God and faith.

A subject he normally avoided like the plague.

"Could we leave earlier than seven?" Naomi's question interrupted his thoughts. "I'd like to take you past the gas station in East Ridge."

Mentally smacking himself on the head for forgetting something so important, he nodded. "Sure thing."

They ate in silence, and when he was finished, he quickly hit the shower and dressed, which took longer than it should have since he had to iron his uniform shirt. When he emerged from his room, he heard the sound of a blow dryer.

He didn't own one but assumed Naomi must have packed one in her duffel bag. Sure enough, five minutes later, she came out of the guest room, carrying her duffel and looking amazing after her turn in the shower.

Despite the small clean bandage she'd applied to her wound, her fresh-faced beauty hit him like a rock between the eyeballs. He tried not to gape like a lovestruck teenager as he stepped forward to take her bag. "Here, I'll carry that for you."

"Thanks."

Oh yeah, he needed some distance from her. Naomi was his witness, not a potential date.

The sooner his brain accepted that fact, the better.

Glancing at the woods bordering his property, he wondered if it would be helpful to search for clues. Not now, but maybe later, while it was still daylight.

Possibly, as he could use all the clues he could find. Yet he couldn't make that a priority at the moment. There was barely enough time to scope out the gas station in East Ridge prior to clocking in for his shift.

And he still needed to find Naomi a safe place to stay.

"Sawyer?"

He glanced at her. "Yeah?"

"Don't you think it's strange that the kidnappers keep coming after me?"

"I do," he admitted. "It's unusual behavior for two men involved in sex trafficking to keep going after one target. Usually, if they get caught trying to snatch one girl, they simply move onto the next."

"That's what I think too." She stared out the window

for a moment. "I could even see how they might be mad at how I escaped, but that seems a lame reason for them to keep coming after me."

"I know." The same thoughts had been bothering him. "You mentioned Kate's father taking off when she was about five. Do you know his name? Or anything about him?"

"His name is Garret Ivy, and I was roughly fifteen when he left." She frowned. "I'm pretty sure he was a car mechanic at a local garage in Dalton. He also liked to stop for a few beers after work. I remember him coming home drunk on occasion."

He made a note to dig into Garret Ivy's background. "So Kate's last name is Ivy?"

"No, our mother never married Garret. Which is why we were so far in debt when he left so abruptly."

He could easily imagine the scenario. "Any idea why he left? Did he and your mother have a fight?"

She grimaced. "I was pretty selfish back then, focused on making the cheerleading squad and being a gymnast. I don't remember a big argument, but they could have had a fight since my mother often asked when he was going to make an honest woman out of her. Personally, I assumed Garret took off because he didn't want anything to do with becoming a husband and a father."

"Any chance he could have come after Kate for some reason?"

She glanced at him in surprise. "It never occurred to me that he would. And honestly, I never got a creepy vibe from him. I can't imagine him being involved in a sex-trafficking ring."

"I know, I was just thinking Garret may have wanted to renew his relationship with Kate. That they could be off somewhere, spending time together."

Naomi bristled. "And what, the white van I followed had nothing to do with my sister being seen leaving work in a white van? What about being rear-ended and kidnapped?"

He held up a hand. "I'm just asking questions, that's all. The way those kidnappers keep coming after you makes it seem very personal."

"I doubt Kate's father is involved."

"Okay, but I had to ask." He slowed to turn toward East Ridge. "Tell me again where this gas station is located?"

She leaned forward, peering through the windshield. "I came in from the other direction, so that means it would be located on the left-hand side of the road."

He swept his gaze over the area. "You were probably closer to the east side of town too, right?"

"Yeah." A small frown furrowed her brow. "It looks so different."

Hopes of her finding the gas station waned. "It's okay if you can't find it."

She didn't answer, still looking around intently.

He continued following the highway, wondering if this was nothing more than a wild goose chase. Even if they found the gas station, it wasn't likely the kidnappers would use the same one again.

Although he did think it was possible the area had been used as a spot to pick up stray girls or hand them off to another driver.

"There! The gas station is up ahead."

He slowed down to turn into the gas station. It wasn't anything fancy; in fact, there wasn't a convenience store to entice drivers to come in to spend more money.

So not a tourist type of gas station, but one used

primarily by the locals. He swung through the parking lot and returned to the main highway.

"When he left the gas station, he went toward the interstate." Naomi waved a hand at the on-ramp. "That way."

Eyeing the time, he decided to follow the same route. He turned and headed onto the interstate. After a few miles, he decided this was pointless and headed off at the nearest exit.

"Sawyer? Isn't that a black Buick?"

"Where?"

Naomi gripped his arm. "I think it went past us on the interstate."

He hesitated, knowing there was more than one black Buick in the area. Then he turned left and went back onto the interstate.

Pressing the gas, he tried to catch up to the traffic up ahead. Sweeping his gaze over the area, he found the Buick.

He moved into the right lane. The black Buick was three cars ahead, making it impossible to see the license plate. He quickly hit the red and blue lights on the top of his squad.

Instantly the car in front of him pulled over, then the next driver did the same. One more vehicle separated him from the Buick when the black car abruptly shot off the exit.

"He's getting away," Naomi cried.

Wrenching the steering wheel, he drove onto the shoulder to go around the idiot who hadn't pulled out of his way. By the time he'd gotten down the exit, he stopped. Had the car gone left or right? He searched the road in both directions.

But there was no sign of the black Buick. It was as if the vehicle had vanished into thin air.

CHAPTER NINE

Naomi tightly gripped the armrest as she listened to Sawyer radioing his dispatcher about following the black Buick and how they'd lost it after exiting the interstate.

So close. They'd been so close to getting Melvin Curtis.

She hadn't been able to get a good look at the license plate, but the way the driver had bolted off the interstate to get away from Sawyer's police vehicle indicated, at least in her mind, criminal intent.

Most drivers pulled over as the first two cars had done. But not the Buick. The driver had taken off and managed to get away rather than pulling over.

She released her grip and glanced at Sawyer. His features were set in a grim expression, and she couldn't blame him for being upset.

Without saying anything, he turned toward downtown Chattanooga. It occurred to her that if she hadn't been in the squad with him, he may have continued searching for the driver of the Buick.

Disheartening, but she wouldn't be in his hair much

longer. Not that she was heading back to Dalton the way he kept suggesting. Instead, she hoped to find a hotel that wouldn't break her bank account.

When he pulled into the parking lot of the precinct, she broke the strained silence. "I'm sorry we lost him."

Sawyer glanced over. "We don't even know that was our guy. But I would have liked to pull him over to find out for sure one way or the other."

"I know." She pushed her car door open. "Hopefully, he sticks around the Chattanooga area long enough for someone to grab him."

"Yeah." Sawyer rested his hand on the small of her back as they went inside. He stopped at the main desk. "Naomi Palmer is here to pick up her driver's license and other personal belongings."

"I believe they're in the lieutenant's office."

"Thanks." Sawyer glanced at her. "Follow me."

Sawyer led the way through the precinct. Like last time, several officers were standing around talking and drinking strong coffee. Sawyer rapped on the door of an office belonging to Evan Watkins.

"Where have you been?" The lieutenant frowned when she followed Sawyer in. "Oh, this must be our witness."

"Lieutenant Watkins, this is Naomi Palmer." Sawyer made the introductions. "Naomi, Lieutenant Watkins is my boss."

"It's nice to meet you, Lieutenant." She offered a smile.

The lieutenant didn't smile back. "Ms. Palmer." He handed her a large bag from his desk. "This is your purse and wallet found at the side of Highway 60."

"Thank you." She opened the evidence bag and pulled out her purse, checking to make sure it was really her driver's license. It was amazing how much better she felt having her ID back. As if she hadn't really existed in the world without it.

Next she pulled out the photograph of Kate. She'd given a copy to the Dalton police and gave this copy to Sawyer. "This is my sister, Kate."

Sawyer gazed at the photograph for a long moment. "I'll make sure copies get to all the squads."

"I'd like that." She was secretly relieved that Sawyer was taking her sister's disappearance so seriously.

More so than the Dalton police had.

"Murphy, I need a word." The lieutenant glanced pointedly at her. "Alone."

"Oh, uh, okay. I'm going. Thanks again." She didn't see any alternative but to leave them alone. She made her way through the building and paused in the police station lobby. Now what? She knew Sawyer would ask her to go back to Dalton, but that wasn't her plan. She stepped outside into the parking lot. Her overnight bag was still in Sawyer's squad, so she went over to grab it.

Being alone in a strange city without a vehicle made her feel vulnerable. But she refused to let fear rule her life. Sawyer had mentioned checking on her Toyota, but that was before he'd gotten into trouble with his boss.

Because of her. It pained her to have put Sawyer in a bad position, but looking back, she didn't know what she could have done differently.

Well, she could help him now by taking care of herself. With her duffel bag looped over her shoulder, she gathered her bearings, creating a map of what little she knew of the city in her head. She walked toward the busiest street, feeling certain that's where most of the hotels would be located.

There were several possibilities, but they looked pricey. She had cash, but it wouldn't last long if she had to spend most of it for a roof over her head.

Traffic whizzed by, and she found herself cringing when she saw a black car. Turned out not to be a Buick. A smaller hotel well off the main drag caught her eye, and she gladly turned down the less busy side street.

As she approached the motel, she realized her ability to get a room this early would be slim to none. Yet she was curious to know their room rate.

Times like this, she missed her smartphone too. There was no way to look up and compare prices on her cheap disposable phone.

The interior lobby of the small motel was cool and dark. When she spoke to the woman behind the desk, Naomi was surprised when the woman agreed to give her a room immediately.

Naomi offered her ID and credit card but quickly added her need to pay in cash. The woman eyed her suspiciously but eventually agreed.

Business must be slow, Naomi thought as she paid for the room. Key in hand, she found her room, wrinkling her nose at the musty smell. She set her bag on the bed and stood for a moment, wondering if she was crazy to stay in the Chattanooga area while the gunman was still on the loose. Then again, it wasn't as if she'd been followed from the police station to the motel.

Her cell phone rang, startling her. Sawyer was the only one who had this number, so she answered it. "Hello?"

"Where are you?" Sawyer's voice was sharp.

"At a motel. Why? What happened with your boss?" She prayed he hadn't lost his job.

"I expected you to wait for me." His tone was more reasonable now. "Which motel?"

She gave him the name, then added, "I don't want you to get in trouble because of me."

"I'll be there in five."

The line went dead. She frowned. What on earth was that about? He'd sounded upset, but he'd known her plan was to stay in Chattanooga.

And why was he coming here anyway? Didn't he have to work?

While she was placing her toiletries in the bathroom, a loud knock echoed at the door. Warily, she peered through the peephole before opening it. "Hey," she greeted him, stepping back so he could enter.

"They gave you a room without a credit card?"

She managed not to roll her eyes. "Obviously."

He turned to face her, his expression somber. "I checked on your car. They've released it for repairs."

"That's great news." She picked up the small notepad and pen from the bedside table. "Can you give me the number so I can call to make arrangements to have it repaired?"

"I've already taken care of it."

She frowned. "Thanks, but I need to know how much so I can repay you."

"Don't worry about it." He waved her off.

She swallowed a wave of impatience. "Sawyer, this is all very nice, but aren't you supposed to be working?"

"Yeah, it's just . . ." He hesitated. "I guess I panicked when I discovered you'd taken off without telling me. I was worried you'd been kidnapped again."

His concern for her welfare was touching, and she felt bad for causing him grief. "I'm sorry. I guess I should have left you a note. Honestly, I feel awful for getting you in trouble with your boss."

Sawyer finally smiled. "Nah. It's not you. He was ticked that I'd followed the black Buick with you in the squad with me, and prior to my shift. But he'll get over it."

Somehow, she knew the discussion had been more serious than Sawyer was telling her, but there wasn't anything she could do to change things now. "Thanks again for everything you've done for me. I won't keep you from your duties."

Sawyer held her gaze for a long moment. "I can't deny you've been a distraction, Naomi. But I need to know you're safe. Please don't take any chances, okay?"

"I won't." She honestly didn't want to go through another kidnapping. Even though she was desperate to find Kate. "And I'll probably call you for an update later."

He stepped closer, his musky scent filling her head with memories of being held in his arms. "I'll probably call you to make sure you're safe."

She was ridiculously pleased to hear that. Her smile faded when Sawyer reached out to pull her into his embrace. Her heart stuttered in her chest when he lowered his head to capture her mouth in a sizzling kiss.

———

SAWYER HAD no idea why he'd kissed his off-limits witness, but once he'd tasted Naomi's sweetness, he couldn't find the strength to let her go.

The way she eagerly participated in the kiss didn't help any. It was only when his radio squawked that he was forced to let her go.

"Ten-four," he said in a hoarse voice. It took a minute to

realize he'd agreed to respond to a call. "I'm sorry, but I have to go."

"Okay." Naomi's breathless voice made him long to kiss her again, until she didn't have the ability to speak at all.

Bad idea. He stepped back and turned toward the door. He had a job to do. One that didn't include kissing Naomi until he couldn't think clearly.

"I'll check in later," he said over his shoulder.

"Okay." Naomi remained exactly where she was, as if unable to move.

He grinned as he left her room to slide in behind the wheel of his squad. It had been a long time since he'd dated anyone. He'd found most women to be clingy and obviously looking for more than he was willing to give. Most women wanted the whole shebang: marriage, a house in a nice neighborhood, 2.5 children, and to hold neighborhood block parties.

Things he didn't want or need.

Yet, for some reason, Naomi didn't intrude on his normal loner mentality.

In fact, he felt off balance without her sitting beside him.

He left the parking lot and headed toward the address the dispatcher had provided. It was a minor miracle that he'd been able to remember anything while cradling Naomi in his arms.

Better to push those thoughts aside. Being distracted while on the job wasn't smart. Domestic incidents, specifically, tended to be some of the most dangerous. Especially since many of the state residents held concealed carry permits.

Thankfully, the disturbance was mild and didn't result in an arrest. In this way, working day shift was nice. Many domestic disputes took place in the late evening hours when heavy drinking was more likely to be involved.

The next call that came through was from Louisa's mother, Francine Marchese. He swung by her house, noting again the close proximity to East Ridge.

"It's almost been a full week," Francine wailed. "Why haven't you found my daughter?"

"Detective Turner has the case," Sawyer reminded her. "I just checked in with him yesterday, and he's still actively searching for Louisa."

"Five days," Francine repeated shrilly. "My baby could be dead!"

He truly felt awful for her. He couldn't imagine what it would be like to lose a child. To not know if your young daughter was dead or alive. "I'm sorry. The entire Chattanooga police force is doing what we can."

She buried her face in her hands, and he gently patted her back. He didn't dare tell her about Kate Palmer also going missing or Naomi's escape from kidnappers suspected of being involved in sex trafficking.

To be honest, Turner pretty much felt Louisa had left on her own with her boyfriend, despite Francine's insistence that her daughter would never do such a thing. Parents didn't always know what their children were capable of.

Yet Sawyer's gut told him Louisa had likely been taken by sex traffickers. When he'd challenged Dewayne Turner, the detective claimed he was keeping an open mind on any and all possibilities, following up on Louisa's boyfriend and her other school friends. From Sawyer's perspective, the guy was wasting time going through that much detail.

Time Louisa didn't have.

After consoling Francine Marchese, Sawyer returned to

his routine patrol, keeping a sharp eye out for any sign of a black Buick and a boxy white van.

The rest of his morning passed with routine calls. He'd dished out a couple of traffic tickets and answered a burglary call.

When he caught a glimpse of a square white van, his heart rate quickened. But then he saw that the side of the van had a logo for a local plumbing company.

Naomi hadn't mentioned seeing a logo on the boxy white van, which he felt certain she couldn't have missed.

It occurred to him that the sex-trafficking ring could add logos to the van as a disguise. If they had done that, it would be impossible to identify the fake logo from a real one.

The black Buick Melvin Curtis owned was their best option of breaking open the case.

Unfortunately, the guy was proving to be as elusive as the mountain mist.

It rankled that the intruder outside his cabin had gotten away. Granted, Sawyer had been shot at twice, which had forced him to slow down. The trip wires he'd placed between the trees had done their job, but not enough to enable him to catch the guy.

It was frustrating to have been this close to grabbing the guy twice, only to fail miserably.

When his stomach rumbled loudly, Sawyer decided to grab fast food for lunch. It made him wonder what Naomi was doing. It was tempting to call and check on her, but he managed to refrain.

His boss had warned him not to let Naomi's kidnapping become a personal vendetta. Especially after hearing about the intruder outside his cabin. Sawyer understood his boss's concern.

A cop needed to keep a clear head when facing danger.

Getting emotionally involved could have a negative impact on his ability to function in a crisis.

Unfortunately, the lieutenant's warning had come too late. He cared about Naomi, more than he should. And her situation of being kidnapped, along with her missing sister, had already become very personal.

He'd barely finished eating his burger when the call about the discovery of a dead body believed to be that of a young girl came over the radio.

Sawyer didn't hesitate. He threw the squad into gear and headed to the location, which happened to be a stone's throw from East Ridge.

That alone had him fearing the worst. Was the dead girl Kate Palmer? Or Louisa Marchese?

Or a completely different young girl who hadn't yet been reported missing?

None of the options were good ones. He detested men who preyed on young girls. When he pulled into the small parking lot, he saw a group of people clustered together off near a thickly wooded area. He quickly shoved his way through them to where another officer, a guy named Brody Jones, was stringing up crime scene tape from tree to tree in an effort to keep the pedestrians and the news media at bay.

"Do you have an ID on the vic?" Sawyer asked.

"No." Brody glanced at him with a grim expression. "Animals have gotten to her, likely coyotes. The condition of the body is not good."

Sawyer swallowed hard, glancing over to an area between two trees where several yellow markers had been placed. "Mind if I take a look?"

Brody shrugged. "Suit yourself, but don't puke on the crime scene."

Sawyer hadn't done that in a long time, but the freshly

eaten burger congealed in his stomach as he carefully moved closer to the victim. This was the absolute worst part of the job, and it never got any easier.

The scene was worse than he imagined. The animals had gotten to her, so there was no way to recognize her face. But he could see a glint of reddish blond hair.

Not Louisa, then. Maybe Kate? He grimaced and pulled the picture Naomi had given him earlier from his pocket.

In the photograph, Kate's hair looked darker than this victim's reddish gold strands. But he couldn't be sure that Naomi's sister hadn't changed her hair color at some point.

What had happened here? He didn't see any clothing, which wasn't something animals normally carried off. Had she tried to run away? Or had she been raped and strangled before being dumped?

It made him sick to think about the terrible fate this young girl had suffered. He turned from the gruesome scene. "Brody? Which detective has this case?"

The cop glanced at him. "Turner is on his way. Although this vic doesn't have dark hair like that missing Marchese girl."

He nodded thoughtfully. "Who found the body?"

"Couple of kids. They ran screaming, bringing several parents out to investigate." Brody shook his head. "No one should have to see that, especially not a little kid."

Sawyer agreed. He showed Brody the picture of Kate. "What do you think? Could this be our vic?"

Brody grimaced. "Maybe. Hard to tell. I'm thinking they'll need dental records and DNA in order to make a positive ID. Unless we're lucky enough that her fingerprints are in the system."

Naomi hadn't mentioned Kate ever being arrested. If

she had, getting a fingerprint match in the system would be helpful. He debated calling Naomi, but then thought better of it.

This wasn't the type of conversation you had over the phone. Bad news was best delivered in person.

CHAPTER TEN

Naomi left her motel room at lunchtime to eat in a café nearby. When she'd finished eating, she didn't want to return to the room. She'd stayed in Chattanooga specifically to help find Kate. Unfortunately, her options were limited without a car.

Walking downtown helped her understand the layout of the city, although she found herself looking frequently over her shoulder. She minimized the risk by sticking with crowds of other tourists. She rather enjoyed seeing the Smoky Mountains, a view she didn't have from her small house in Dalton. Yet as much as she liked the area, her primary concern was to find the boxy white van or the black Buick.

Neither vehicle was likely to be spotted by her walking along the side of the road. After escaping the kidnappers, Sawyer had accused her of using herself as bait. Which, frankly, she had.

Being outside in the open for anyone to see made her feel like that again. And honestly? She didn't like it. The idea of being captured and held by the kidnappers for a second time made her stomach twist with fear.

But how else would she find out what had happened to her sister?

Naomi sent up a silent prayer for God to continue guiding her on this journey. To keep Kate safe from harm and to bring her sister home.

Only this time, she didn't experience the reassuring sense of peace.

Naomi wasn't sure how long she wandered around Chattanooga, but she suddenly stopped when she realized her surroundings were not at all familiar.

With a sigh of disgust, she was forced to admit she'd gotten lost.

"Idiot," she muttered. She pulled out her phone to call Sawyer, frowning when she realized the disposable phone screen was blank.

Had she accidentally turned the phone off? Or had the battery died?

Naomi attempted to power up the phone without success. Feeling foolish for being irresponsible, she glanced around for a pay phone to use. There wasn't one anywhere in sight; however, a police squad pulled up next to the curb. Recognizing Sawyer behind the wheel, she approached the passenger side as he lowered the window.

"Where have you been?" His harsh tone instantly put her back up.

"Walking, why? Is that a crime?"

"Of course not, but I've been calling you without an answer. I was worried something bad happened to you."

"I'm sorry." She flushed, realizing he had a right to be concerned. "I didn't realize my phone battery died."

He sighed and gestured for her to get in. The interior of the squad was amazingly cool compared to the sticky summer heat. "I hope you weren't driving around looking for me."

"That's exactly what I've been doing." Sawyer still sounded irked.

"I'm sorry," she repeated. What more could she say? It wasn't as if she'd cut off all communication with him on purpose.

"Has Kate ever been arrested?"

Sawyer's question came from the stratosphere. "What? Why?"

"Please, Naomi." His dark gaze was compelling. "Just tell me if she has or hasn't."

"Never." She eyed him warily as he navigated the traffic to head back to her motel. The area looked familiar now, so she must not have been too far off track.

"I have bad news," Sawyer said slowly. "And I need you to understand we don't have a positive ID yet."

A chill snaked down her spine. She gripped the armrest of the car door. "You found Kate?"

"No, as I mentioned, we don't have a positive ID," Sawyer said firmly. "But a young girl is dead. And she isn't Louisa."

Dead.

The word hit her hard, despite his insistence there was no positive ID. He wouldn't be telling her this if he wasn't concerned that the dead girl could very well be Kate.

"I need to see her."

"No, you don't," Sawyer swiftly countered. "Trust me on this. The unknown female victim was left in the woods where the wildlife has gotten to her. There isn't a way to make a positive ID except by fingerprints, and if that doesn't work, dental records."

Her stomach lurched, and she had to swallow the urge to throw up. This was the news she'd dreaded since the moment she'd known Kate was missing.

She squeezed her eyes shut, trying not to imagine a ravaged Kate being found in the woods.

"Naomi, please don't do this." Sawyer's voice was softly pleading. "I only mentioned it because if we don't get a match on a set of fingerprints in the system, we'll need to look at dental records. Kate's records."

Her stomach lurched again, and she pressed her hand to her abdomen. She took several deep breaths before she could manage to speak. "I can get in touch with our dentist in town."

"That would be helpful," Sawyer admitted. "Any chance your sister may have dyed her hair? The color on our girl in the woods doesn't exactly match your sister's from what I can tell."

A surge of hope hit hard. "Not that I know of. So the girl in the woods may not be Kate?"

"I warned you that we didn't have a positive ID." Sawyer reached over to take her hand. "For your sake, I hope our unknown female isn't Kate. But we'll need to find out for sure one way or the other."

She gripped his hand tightly and nodded. "Okay."

Sawyer drove her back to her motel room. Rummaging in her duffel bag, she found the phone charging cord and plugged it in.

"Here, use mine." He handed over his smartphone. "I'm sure you don't know your dentist's number by heart."

"I don't." Taking his phone, she performed a quick search for Dr. Lee Radtke in Dalton. With trembling fingers, she punched in the phone number.

"Dr. Radtke's office, can I help you?"

"This is Naomi Palmer. I'm, uh, calling about dental records for my sister, Kate Palmer. She's missing, and the Chattanooga police need them to . . ." She couldn't finish.

Sawyer took the phone from her hand. "This is Officer Sawyer Murphy from the Chattanooga PD. We have an unknown female victim that we'd like to identify. Kate Palmer has been missing for several days. I have her guardian, Naomi Palmer, here. If you could send a copy of Kate's dental records to our precinct, we can use them to help us identify the victim."

Naomi couldn't hear what the response was, but when Sawyer rattled off a fax number, she knew they were willing to cooperate.

Her knees went weak. She sank down onto the edge of the bed, her mind spinning. Was this why she hadn't felt God's peace earlier? Because her sister was already dead?

Sawyer sank down beside her and put his arm around her shoulders. Grateful, she leaned against him.

"I'm sorry, Naomi." He kissed her uninjured temple.

She nodded. "H-how long does it take to complete the process of identifying the girl?"

There was a brief pause. "I'm not sure," he admitted. "But she's been taken to the morgue where they'll do an autopsy. We should hear something once they're able to check her fingerprints for a match in the system and have a chance to review her dental records."

Her beautiful, outgoing younger sister might be lying on a cold metal table in the morgue. It was all so surreal. So inconceivable. This kind of thing didn't happen in Dalton, Georgia. Naomi's job as a clinic nurse was mundane. Her life was centered around providing a stable home for Kate. They'd even planned to visit some colleges in the fall. Kate had expressed a desire to go to Tennessee, while Naomi had hoped she'd attend Georgia State to save money on tuition.

Then Kate had disappeared, and Naomi had been kidnapped.

The thought of burying her sister beside her mother made her eyes well with tears.

Why, God, why?

There was no answer.

DESPITE HIS WARNINGS to the contrary, Sawyer knew Naomi was imagining the worst.

That her half sister was dead.

He wished he could assure her otherwise, but he couldn't. He'd debated telling Naomi anything at all about the girl they'd found. Yet on a practical level, having Kate's dental records would help, especially since he'd had a bad feeling their unknown female victim's fingerprints wouldn't pop in AFIS, the Automated Fingerprint Identification System law enforcement had access to.

The hour he hadn't been able to find Naomi had been the worst thing he'd endured since escaping the Preacher. And that was saying a lot. He'd done the same thing she was doing, imagining the worst-case scenario, while fruitlessly searching for her. When he'd caught a glimpse of Naomi strolling along without a care in the world, he'd hit the brakes so hard he'd nearly caused a chain reaction collision.

He'd mentally thanked God for keeping Naomi safe before he could stop himself.

If there really was a God, He wouldn't listen to him, not after what Sawyer had done thirteen years ago.

"What about her clothing?" Naomi's abrupt question

pulled him from his dark thoughts. "I'm sure I could recognize what she was wearing."

Oh boy. He tightened his grip around her shoulders. "I'm sorry, but we didn't find any clothing."

She gasped. "Naked? She was found naked?"

"Yes. But we don't know that the girl is Kate." He sounded like a broken record, but he understood she was upset. "Please try not to go down that path, Naomi."

"Even if she's not Kate, she's still someone's daughter, sister, or friend." Her voice was so soft he could barely hear her. "She didn't deserve to be left naked in the woods."

"I know." The crime scene would haunt him for a long time too. And he found himself hoping that his foster sisters Darby, Jayme, and Caitlyn hadn't suffered a similar fate.

In that respect, he'd been fortunate to have had Joseph Kohl pull him off the streets. Offering food and shelter with no strings attached. After a few months of living together, the cop admitted to losing his wife after four years of marriage. When Sawyer asked why he wasn't seeing anyone now, Joe had claimed Sharon had been his soul mate and irreplaceable. Then Joe had gone on to tell Sawyer he was the son he and Sharon had never had.

Sawyer was touched by his confession and had done everything in his power to make Joe proud. Including letting go of his anger toward the Preacher.

Naomi abruptly turned and buried her face in the hollow of his shoulder. Sobs racked her body, tears dampening his shirt. He held her close, wishing there was more he could do. Ignoring the desire to kiss her, he continued offering comfort and support until she'd pulled herself together.

She sniffled and pushed away, swiping at her face. "Sorry for blubbering."

"No reason to apologize," he assured her.

She shrugged and sniffed again. "I'm sure you have to get back to work, but will you call me when you hear something?"

"Yes, but keep your phone on, okay?"

She grimaced. "I will. And I'll stay here, if that helps."

"I only have another ninety minutes to go. I'll swing by once I'm off duty."

"I'd appreciate that, thanks." Her expression was still ragged, but he admired her attempt to remain strong.

He pressed a chaste kiss to the top of her head and stood. "Hang in there, okay? I'll be in touch soon."

"I will." She followed him to the door. He could feel her gaze on him as he slid behind the wheel of the squad.

Leaving her in the motel room wasn't easy, and it occurred to him that he wouldn't be able to stand having her spend the night here in the motel while he was sleeping twenty minutes outside of town in his cabin.

Yeah, he was in trouble. Big, big trouble.

And worst of all, he had no desire to be rescued.

As he merged into traffic, he heard another call come through the radio. It was the dispatcher calling him specifically.

"Dispatch, this is unit seven responding."

"A fax came through with your name on it, Officer Murphy," the dispatcher informed him.

He was glad to hear Naomi's dentist had worked so fast. "Do me a favor and send a copy to Detective Turner and to the medical examiner's office. The records belong to Kate Palmer, a missing sixteen-year-old girl from Dalton, Georgia. I need them compared to our unknown female."

"I'll take care of it," the dispatcher assured him.

"Ten-four." He hoped Naomi would get good news sooner rather than later.

The last hour of his shift passed in what felt like slow motion. He'd pulled over another speeder, but even that hadn't helped make the time go by faster. Finally, it was close enough to four o'clock that he could return to the precinct.

The first thing he did was find Detective Turner. The guy was sitting at his desk, which irked Sawyer for some reason. "Detective? Did you get the dental records I sent?"

"Yeah." Dewayne Turner sighed. "Thanks for getting them. I'm working as fast as I can."

He was? Could have fooled him. Sawyer strove for patience. "I can help. Naomi Palmer has been searching for her sister, Kate. I can find out if her dental records are a match to the victim found earlier today."

"That really isn't your job," Turner pointed out. Although Sawyer noticed he didn't sound irritated by his butting into the case. "I haven't heard anything from the ME's office yet."

Sawyer decided to tread softly. "Would you mind if I made a few phone calls?"

"I can't stop you. I'm going through Louisa's phone records." Turner turned his gaze back to his computer. Phone records? Sawyer wanted to point out that doing that task was fruitless, but he held his tongue.

For now, he'd focus on giving their young female victim a name.

Sawyer returned to one of the general-use cubicles and picked up the phone. He dialed the ME's office, relieved when someone quickly answered.

"This is Officer Murphy checking in on the ID for the unknown female victim found earlier today."

"Uh, yes, officer. I see you sent dental records to compare to the victim. Unfortunately, the medical examiner hasn't gotten to them yet. He's still working on cause of death."

Cause of death was important, but Sawyer doubted the ME would be able to say anything with certainty, considering the condition of the body. Yet the ME no doubt had a methodical approach to his work, one Sawyer didn't want to mess around with.

"Any idea when he'll have a chance to make the comparison? I have the sister of a missing teenager here, waiting to hear the news one way or the other."

"Hopefully by the end of the day."

It was better than he'd expected. "Thanks. If you don't mind, I'll check back later then."

"Fine with me."

Sawyer set his phone aside and sat back in his chair. He tried to understand what was going on with Turner. The guy had gotten the gold shield instead of Sawyer due to scoring two points higher on the detective's exam and having nearly five years of seniority. Was it possible Turner wasn't capable of doing the job? The guy seemed to be getting lost in the details instead of focusing on the big picture. It wasn't as if dead bodies of young girls showed up on a regular basis. This was the first in the past eighteen months.

Something this serious usually took precedence over everything else. So why wasn't Turner putting in a bigger effort to find out what happened? The guy hadn't even bothered to talk to Naomi directly but had taken the information Sawyer had provided as if that was good enough.

Sawyer considered going to the lieutenant with his concerns but knew his boss would only reiterate his earlier order not to let this case become personal. And maybe he was. Louisa's mother deserved his best work.

As did Naomi.

After drawing his hands over his face to combat a wave of exhaustion, he left the police station. Outside, he hesitated. Rather than using his squad, he crossed over to where he'd left his personal vehicle, a gray SUV. Using the squad to go back and forth to work was one of the few perks their boss readily allowed.

But after the intruder had shown up last night, Sawyer decided against using the same squad he'd been driving the past few days. The only way he could imagine being found was by the squad's license plate number.

Using his personal SUV should help provide anonymity while he was on the road.

Unfortunately, the intruder already knew where he lived. Which made going back to the cabin a bad idea.

Or a good one, if he could find a way to set a trap.

He mulled over that idea as he returned to the motel. He stopped in the lobby long enough to get a second room, right next to Naomi's. They weren't connecting rooms, but it was better than nothing.

He entered his room first, checking the place out. The added bonus to having his own SUV was that he carried a change of clothing. His boss didn't like his officers being in uniform while off duty. He grabbed his bag and quickly changed before going over to knock lightly on Naomi's door.

"Any news?" she asked expectantly.

"Not yet." Her face fell. "The medical examiner has your sister's dental records. We will hopefully hear something in the next hour or so."

"Okay, thanks." Her attempt to smile was pathetic. "I haven't been able to think of anything else," she added in an apologetic tone. "I feel like I'm frozen in time. That I can't move forward without knowing if that poor girl is Kate."

"I understand." He held up his room key. "I'm right next door if you need anything."

"Really?" Her expression brightened. "You're staying here too?"

He nodded. "Figured it was the least I could do."

"Oh, Sawyer." To his horror, her blue eyes filled with tears. "I don't know what I'd do without you."

"Hey, don't cry." He awkwardly patted her back, feeling a bit at a loss. It was one thing for her to cry over her sister, but to cry because he'd done something she viewed as nice? He didn't like that. "It's my job to help find your sister. And to keep you safe."

"I'm sorry." She turned away and grabbed a tissue. She blew her nose, then added, "It's been a rough day."

"I know." It was a bit early to eat dinner, but he thought it would be good for her to get out of the motel room. "Let's find someplace to eat."

Naomi hesitated, then nodded. "Okay, let me get my phone."

"There's a family restaurant across the street," he said as she removed her phone from the charger.

"I know, I ate there for lunch." She glanced at him. "I don't mind going back."

"Okay." He preferred staying close to the motel. "We can walk, if you don't mind."

The restaurant wasn't busy. He and Naomi were given a booth in the corner, and he sat where he could keep an eye on the door.

"I'm not that hungry," Naomi said, glancing briefly at the menu.

"Try to eat something." He didn't want to call the ME's

office again until the hour was close to five o'clock. No sense in being a pest. "Keep up your strength."

She wrinkled her nose. "I'll try the soup, then."

"How's your headache?"

"Better, thanks."

Once they'd ordered their meals, Naomi asked, "Is the medical examiner going to call you?"

"I'm supposed to check back at five." He didn't mention anything about his frustration with the detective. "They have my number as well."

She stared down at her water for a long moment. "I keep going back and forth. If Kate is gone, I'd rather know now than be in limbo for years. But I don't want to lose her, Sawyer." She lifted her gaze to his. "She's all the family I have left."

It was on the tip of his tongue to tell her about his foster family, about how they'd lost touch after escaping the Preacher. His attention was diverted to his ringing phone.

"Murphy," he answered. Naomi froze, her gaze boring into his.

"This is the ME's office. Dr. Watterson wanted me to tell you the dental records you sent through earlier are not a match."

"The dental records are not a match? Okay, thank you." His shoulders sagged in relief. The unknown female victim wasn't Kate. Or Louisa.

Which meant they had a third missing girl on their hands. Another victim of sex trafficking? Highly likely.

And their only suspects, Melvin Curtis and Naomi's leering man, still haven't been found.

CHAPTER ELEVEN

Not a match. The dead girl wasn't her sister. Naomi was ashamed at the faint sense of disappointment she'd felt upon hearing the dead girl wasn't Kate.

Of course, she didn't want Kate to be dead. As she'd told Sawyer, her sister was the only family she had left. But she also didn't want her sister to suffer. And logically Naomi knew the longer it took for them to find Kate, the less likely they'd succeed.

And the more her sister would suffer unspeakable sexual abuse.

It was impossible to imagine never knowing where Kate was. If her sister was alive or dead. Stuck in some horrible situation or had gotten free but had decided for some reason not to return home.

The myriad of emotions made her head hurt more than usual. She pushed the pain away to focus on Sawyer. "If the girl you found isn't Kate or Louisa, then who is she?"

He shook his head. "I don't know. I haven't heard about another missing girl from the area, but it could very well be that the girl is missing from out of state. North Carolina or

Georgia." He shrugged. "Could be from anywhere, honestly, if East Ridge is indeed some sort of hub for sex traffickers."

She abruptly straightened in her seat. "Shouldn't the FBI be involved? If these girls are being trafficked across state lines, the crime would be prosecuted at a federal level, right?"

"Yes, it would. I need to discuss this with my boss. The detective on the case should already be in contact with the local FBI office here in Chattanooga considering you and your sister are both from Georgia. There are only a couple of lower level agents working here in town, the special agent in charge works out of the Knoxville office."

"Maybe I should go to the local FBI office to talk with them directly," she said, more to herself than to Sawyer.

"It's too late today, but I can take you there tomorrow," he offered.

Tomorrow was Friday, and she knew the office wasn't likely open on the weekend. "Okay, that sounds good." She fell silent as their server brought their meals. Her appetite had vanished, but she'd need to eat to keep up her strength.

When she realized Sawyer was waiting for her to pray, she clasped her hands together in her lap and bent her head. "Lord, we thank You for this food we are about to eat. And we ask You to show us the way to rescuing Kate and Louisa. Amen."

To her surprise, Sawyer echoed, "Amen."

She was humbled that he'd participated in her prayer and found her appetite had returned. She gratefully took a bite of her thick and tasty clam chowder.

"We need to find Melvin Curtis or the guy on the sketch," Sawyer said softly.

She glanced up at him. "Do you think one of them is the gunman?"

"Yeah, I do. It's the only thing that makes sense." He took a large bite of his burger.

"I seem to be their target." She stared out the window of the restaurant. They'd kidnapped her once, and she hated to admit how scary it would be to have them succeed in grabbing her a second time.

"No." Sawyer's tone was curt. "Don't even think of setting yourself up as bait to draw them out."

She pushed aside her fear. "I'm sure it would work fine if you and several police officers were hiding nearby, ready to take them down."

"No way, Naomi." Sawyer's expression turned grim. "Setting something up would be more complicated than that. These guys aren't stupid. They wouldn't just come after you while you were sitting out in the open, that would be too obvious. And trying to set up something while you're on the move at night would be incredibly risky."

He had a point, but she was far from satisfied. "If not that, then what?" she asked in frustration. "There must be something we can do to catch them."

Sawyer didn't answer. She tried not to snap at him, but her patience was wearing thin.

Her sister was still missing. Naomi believed in God but knew that faith alone wasn't going to get them through this.

God helps those who help themselves.

"What did you say?" Sawyer asked.

She glanced up in surprise. Had she said those words out loud? Flustered, she waved a hand. "God helps those who help themselves. Although the actual phrase from the Bible in the book of Psalms is: *The Lord is with me; he is my helper.*"

Sawyer stared at her for a long moment. "I've never heard that phrase before."

She eyed him thoughtfully. "I know you've mentioned not believing in God, but it seems as if you've been exposed to some religion."

"More like exposed to evil," Sawyer said bluntly. "That foster home I mentioned? I lived there with six other kids with a man who called himself the Preacher. Only he was the exact opposite of what most people consider God to be like."

"I'm sorry to hear that." She frowned and took another sip of her soup. "But if you actually read the Bible, you'd learn that God is kind, compassionate, and forgiving."

"Forgiving?" He didn't look convinced. "I doubt that."

"Remember, God sent Jesus to die for our sins." This was the second time he'd referred to some sins being too much for God to forgive. "And none of us are innocent."

He didn't say anything more but concentrated on his food. Still, she felt as if she may have gained some ground with him. It hurt that Sawyer didn't believe he was good enough.

"Sawyer?"

He glanced up at her. "Yeah?"

"I'm sorry you had such a terrible experience with someone pretending to do God's work, but I want you to know you're the nicest guy I've ever met."

He glanced away, and she thought she noticed a dark flush creep into his cheeks. "You must not meet very many guys," he said lightly. "Or you're comparing me to the likes of Melvin Curtis and leering man."

"That's not true. I dated a guy named Tony Baldwin. He pressured me for more than I was comfortable with, then issued an ultimatum. Sleep with him or lose him. I walked away."

Sawyer scowled. "He sounds like a jerk."

She smiled. "He is, but you aren't. That's what I'm trying to say. Give yourself a break, Sawyer. No one is perfect, and God loves us anyway."

"I'll try." It wasn't a strong conviction, but it wasn't a refusal either. She decided to believe Sawyer was taking a step in the right direction.

When they finished eating, Sawyer waved their server over to pay the bill. She pulled out some money, but he frowned and shook his head.

"My treat, Naomi. Save your money for the motel room and other necessities."

More proof that Sawyer was a far better man than Tony Baldwin. Even while they were dating, Tony would sometimes ask her to pay, claiming he was short on cash. Yet she'd find out later that, after dropping her off at home, he'd gone to the bar with his friends.

Whatever. Tony wasn't worth a minute of time. She was better off without him.

"Thank you for dinner." She glanced over her shoulder as Sawyer held the door for her.

Clouds had gathered overhead while they'd eaten, bringing the threat of a thunderstorm. When Sawyer turned toward the motel, she put a hand on his arm to stop him.

"What's wrong?"

"Nothing, but I'd like to see the area where the girl's body was found."

He frowned. "That's not a good idea. It's still a crime scene."

"We won't do anything to harm evidence, but I keep

thinking of the possibility that Kate managed to escape her captors. She could be held somewhere near the location of the dead girl."

"There's no evidence the girl was running away." He glanced off in the distance. "In fact, the techs are thinking her body may have been dumped there."

Her stomach lurched. "But you don't know for sure, right?"

"Nothing has been confirmed."

"Then what's the harm in going over there? I just want to see the area for myself."

"I don't think it will help," he warned.

"Please, Sawyer." She held his gaze, willing him to go along with her plan. "I need to do something. It's too early to sit in the motel room for the rest of the night."

He blew out a frustrated breath. "Okay, fine. I'll take you there. But don't blame me if you have nightmares."

"My nightmares are centered on being run off the road and kidnapped." And of Kate being held captive, but she decided against mentioning that.

He winced and rested his hand in the small of her back. "I'm sorry, I know how traumatic that must have been. I've had nightmares about the time we spent with the Preacher too. Trust me when I say they get less frequent over time."

"Nightmares about the Preacher?" She frowned. "Was he abusive in some way?"

"A bit." He quickly changed the subject. "Okay, I'll take you past the crime scene, but we're not going close. We'll take my SUV, it's parked at the motel."

She wanted to press for more but let it go. "Thanks." She walked toward a gray SUV. "What happened to the squad?"

"Left it at the precinct. My personal vehicle will give us more anonymity."

She understood he was talking about the way the intruder had found them at his cabin. His private space, which should have been a safe haven rather than a place where he'd been shot at. "I hate knowing you've been dragged into this with me."

"I volunteered to be a part of this to help you, Naomi. And I'd do it again." Pulling the key fob from his pocket, he unlocked the vehicle.

She slid into the passenger seat, knowing God had sent Sawyer to help her.

Hopefully, she could help Sawyer in return.

At least she understood now why he didn't have a relationship with God. Maybe that was part of her purpose here.

Along with helping to find Kate.

As Sawyer navigated the city streets, she searched for any sign of the black Buick, the driver, and leering man. A horrible thought hit, and she turned toward him. "What if the news of the girl's body being found here causes the kidnappers to leave the state?"

"That's a possibility," he agreed. "Although I doubt the media knows many details about the situation. Especially since law enforcement doesn't know very much, including the girl's identity."

"But if the kidnappers knew they'd dumped a body there, wouldn't they be running scared?" She swept her gaze over the area, taking note of how remote the location was from the residential part of town. "They could be long gone, which means we'll never catch them."

"Try not to think the worst," Sawyer said reassuringly. "These guys haven't acted logically since kidnapping you.

They should have left right away once you escaped, but they didn't. They recklessly took a shot at you, then came to my cabin to do the same."

She wasn't convinced. "You mentioned this seemed personal." Another terrible thought struck her. "What if Kate's father, Garret Ivy, didn't try to reconnect with her? What if he took her someplace? What if you were right and he really is somehow involved in this?"

"He took off when Kate was only five, right?" Sawyer glanced at her. "What would make him come back after all this time?"

"Maybe he knew our mother passed away. And that was enough to make him return to reunite with Kate. Only she didn't want to go, so he forced her."

"If that's the case, there's no reason to hurt her."

"I don't know about that." Her memory of Kate's father was that of a drunk with grease-stained fingers. "Garret never had enough money, except he managed to drink to excess more often than not."

She forced herself to consider the possibility that Garret Ivy could have gotten involved with criminals over the past eleven years. She hadn't been creeped out by him when she was young, but things could change. Maybe now he was teamed up with a group of men who preyed on young women?

What if Garret helped drag his own daughter into a sex-trafficking ring?

And was determined to silence Naomi because she would be able to recognize him?

NAOMI HAD GONE PALE, and it didn't take much effort on his part to realize she was once more thinking the worst.

"We don't have any evidence that the kidnappers have connections with Garret Ivy," he said, voicing her obvious concern.

"You were the one who mentioned these attempts on me seemed personal," Naomi pointed out. "And you mentioned Garret being a suspect earlier."

"I know." He had to admit that despite the lack of proof, the possible connection made sense. Catching a glimpse of yellow crime scene tape up ahead, he slowed down and searched for a place to pull over.

"Is that it?" She peered through the windshield. "I thought she was found closer to the road."

"No, twenty yards off the road, in the woods." Why had he given in to her wish to come here? It was a bad idea.

"Can we walk over there?"

"No. For many reasons, as I said, we can't contaminate the crime scene. Besides, the officers who responded to the scene did a sweep of the area without finding anything significant. There's nothing out there for you to see."

"It's relatively close to East Ridge."

"But not within the city limits."

She shot him a frustrated look. "I saw the black Buick in East Ridge, which means they're familiar with the area. And they could also be staying in the area. Maybe we should walk around outside the yellow tape area, see if we can find something?"

Find something? He suppressed a sigh. "Naomi, all the officers on patrol are looking for Melvin Curtis and the leering man, they have the sketch you helped create. If they're hanging out here, we'll find them."

"Yeah, except it's already been two days without

anything." She turned away from him to look out at the crime scene. "I don't know, Sawyer. It feels like the location of this poor girl's body should be significant."

"I hear you." He understood her frustration. "And once we have the men in custody, we'll know more." At least, he certainly hoped so.

He merged back into traffic, looking for a spot to get off the highway to turn around. Being in East Ridge bothered him, although there was no logical reason for him to feel that way.

Yet his priority was to keep Naomi safe, and that meant getting her back to the motel.

"Would you mind stopping at the gas station up ahead?" Naomi glanced at him, her expression embarrassed. "I'm sorry, but I need to use the restroom."

"Sure." It wouldn't hurt to add fuel to his tank as there was less than a quarter remaining. The gas station she'd pointed out was as good a place as any. He frowned when he noticed a small sign indicating they were entering East Ridge.

The gas station and convenience store wasn't anywhere close to the one where Naomi had seen Melvin Curtis. Still, he kept a sharp eye out for anything unusual as he drove into the small lot and pulled up in front of the closest fuel pump.

"Thanks again," she said, pushing her door open. As he pumped gas, Naomi disappeared inside the building. He fought the urge to call her back, insisting she wait for him.

A flash of lightning lit up the sky, followed by the rolling sound of thunder. Glancing up at the swirling clouds overhead, he suspected a deluge of rain wasn't far behind.

The dark storm clouds masked the descent of the sun over the western ridge of the Smoky Mountains, making the hour seem later than it was. He turned to watch the doorway for Naomi, frowning when he didn't see her.

Was she still in the bathroom? Or was she shopping for something she'd forgotten to pack? He told himself there was no reason to be concerned, he'd just go inside to meet up with her. When he finished topping off his tank, he replaced the pump and stuck the receipt in his pocket.

Before he could head inside, his phone rang. Glancing at the screen, his frown cleared when he saw Naomi's number. "What's up? You get lost in the store?"

No response.

Had she pocket dialed him? No, it wouldn't be easy to do that with a disposable phone.

His blood ran cold, and every one of his senses flashed in warning.

Something was wrong.

He swept his gaze over the area, but it wasn't easy to see in the dim light. Had someone grabbed her? Melvin Curtis? Or leering man?

He slid his phone into his pocket, then removed his weapon from his belt holster. Holding his gun at the ready, he edged along his SUV, looking toward the rear of the gas station.

There was a cluster of trees along the back of the gas station. The wind picked up, causing the branches to sway back and forth.

But then he caught a glimpse of pale skin between the rustling leaves.

Naomi!

Without hesitating, he ran silently toward the cluster of trees. He wasn't wearing his uniform, so he couldn't radio for backup. And he wasn't willing to use his phone, breaking the only connection he might have to her.

Pressing his back up against the side of the building, he paused and waited for more movement. The seconds went by with excruciating slowness, until he thought he'd go crazy if he had to wait much longer.

There! A tree branch snapped into place, and he thought he heard a muffled thud.

He eased into the brush, his gaze pinned on the area where he'd seen movement. Quickening his pace, he burst through the foliage and stumbled into the other side of the cluster of trees, horrified to find Naomi being held at gunpoint by a burly man who resembled the grainy driver's license photo of Melvin Curtis.

"Police!" Sawyer shouted loudly, hoping someone nearby would call 911. "Drop your weapon and put your hands where I can see them!"

Melvin didn't move. Another flash of lightning brightened the sky, revealing the burly man's evil eyes. For a moment he could have sworn Melvin was the Preacher.

"Stay back or I'll kill her."

On the heels of Melvin's threat came more rolling thunder. Sawyer kept his gun trained on Melvin when Naomi abruptly broke free, diving toward the ground to her left.

Incensed, Melvin moved the barrel of his gun toward her. Without hesitation, Sawyer shot twice, hitting the guy in the upper part of his chest. Melvin's eyes widened in shock as he stumbled backward from the impact of the bullets.

The clouds overhead opened up, dumping a barrage of rain. Visibility was awful, and he lost sight of Naomi.

"Naomi!" His shout was muffled by the rain.

"Here! I'm here." She lunged to her feet and came rushing toward him.

"Get behind me," he ordered. He stared at Melvin

Curtis lying on the ground. The idiot still had his gun in hand. "Melvin Curtis, drop your weapon!"

The man didn't let go of the gun.

Sawyer feared the guy would die before they had a chance to question him. "Drop the gun!"

The weapon finally fell from Melvin's lifeless fingers. Sawyer rushed forward but instinctively knew it was too late. His aim had been true.

Melvin Curtis was dead.

CHAPTER TWELVE

Naomi wrapped her arms around her body, shivering in the rain as Sawyer knelt beside Melvin Curtis. The sound of sirens filled the air, and she could see the flash of red lights in the distance.

The temperatures weren't bad, in the midseventies, but she couldn't seem to stop shaking. She'd stepped out of the bathroom straight into the driver of the Buick. By the time she'd recognized him, he'd jammed his gun into her side.

She'd managed to call Sawyer with one hand deep in her pocket, but she couldn't tell him what was happening. And when she'd heard Sawyer shouting at Melvin to drop the gun, she'd feared the guy was going to kill her right then and there.

Her teeth began to chatter uncontrollably, her shaking intensifying. Her feet were glued to the ground. She couldn't move. Couldn't speak.

She'd thought she was going to die.

Thank you, Lord, for sparing me!

The prayer popped into her head, and her trembling

eased. She drew in a deep breath and managed to move toward Sawyer and the dead man.

"Are you hurt?" he asked when she approached.

"N-no." She stared at the unmoving body of Melvin Curtis. "Thank you for saving my life."

"You were the one who managed to get away from him." Sawyer stared through the rain at her. "I couldn't believe it when you went down."

"I took advantage of the moment you distracted him." She pushed her sopping wet hair from her face. "But if you hadn't found us, I'd be dead."

Another chill rippled down her spine.

Sawyer rose and came over to hug her. They were both drenched, but she clung to him, burying her face in the hollow of his neck.

Sawyer might not believe it, but she knew God had been with them the whole time, keeping them safe.

"I was so scared he'd hurt you, Naomi," he murmured in her ear. "And I'm not sure how I managed to find you."

"God was guiding you. And me." She felt his muscles stiffen for a moment before he relaxed.

"You could be right," he admitted. "Because it seemed as if I was being pushed toward you."

That he'd even admitted that much filled her heart with hope. "Trust in Him, Sawyer."

"I'm trying." The sirens grew louder, the red lights brighter. Sawyer loosened his grip, and she immediately missed his warmth. "Backup has arrived."

A bit late, but better now than never. Glancing back over at Melvin, she belatedly realized Sawyer might be in serious trouble over shooting and killing him.

Two officers came toward Sawyer. He held up his badge. "I'm an off-duty cop."

"Murphy? Is that you?" The larger of the two men squinted through the rain.

"Yeah, it's me. I shot Melvin Curtis to protect victim Naomi Palmer."

The cop's flashlight illuminated her face, before going back to Sawyer. "Okay, you know the drill."

"I do." Sawyer carefully handed over his weapon. "You'll find Curtis's gun on the ground beside him. He wouldn't let go of the weapon, making it impossible for me to render first aid."

"He threatened to kill me." Naomi wanted the police officers to understand the gravity of the situation. "I—I thought for sure I was going to die."

"Ma'am? We're going to need you to come down to the police station to give your statement." It wasn't easy to read his name tag through the dark rain, but she thought his last name was Finley. "Why don't you wait in the back of my squad?"

She hesitated, unwilling to be separated from Sawyer. He'd become her lifeline over the past few days. It probably wasn't healthy, but she didn't like being far from him.

"Go on," Sawyer encouraged. "May as well get out of the rain."

"I have a blanket," Finley added. He pointed at the car parked behind them. "This way, please."

Naomi reluctantly allowed the officer to lead her from the crime scene. The blanket he gave her was nice, but sitting in the back seat of the squad, watching as the officers moved around the area behind the gas station, brought the memories back.

She should have recognized Melvin Curtis sooner. Should have managed to get away from him before he'd dragged her out of the rear door of the gas station.

Before Sawyer had to shoot him.

Now Melvin was dead, and they still didn't know where Kate was or if he was actually involved in her disappearance.

She'd handled things badly. And the people who would suffer the most from her mistakes were Kate, Louisa, and Sawyer.

Her breathing quickly fogged up the windows to the point she couldn't see anything that was happening. When her door abruptly opened, she reared back in surprise.

"Ms. Palmer?" Officer Finley gave her a look of sympathy. "The EMTs would like to examine you."

"I'm not hurt." She'd dove to the ground, rolling away from Melvin Curtis on her own. There had been some gravel in the palms of her hand, but nothing serious. "I don't need to be examined, thanks."

"Are you sure?" Officer Finley didn't look convinced. "You've suffered an emotional trauma."

That was one way to put it. But she didn't want to be taken to the hospital either. Her headache lingered but was nothing in comparison to nearly being shot to death. "I'm a critical care nurse and can assure you I'm fine." She forced a smile. "I promise."

"Okay, but if you change your mind, let me know." He slammed the car door shut.

She blew out a breath and wondered how Sawyer was holding up. He'd saved her life twice now. She was grateful God had sent Sawyer to help her.

Yet she worried Sawyer wouldn't be able to shake off the fact that he'd killed a man. Even a lowlife like Melvin Curtis. Even when he'd only shot him to protect her.

She felt terrible about putting him in that situation and

couldn't help but wonder if Sawyer had been forced to shoot someone in self-defense before today.

Not that it would matter. Each time he was forced to use deadly force had to take an emotional toll.

Closing her eyes, she prayed God would bring Sawyer peace and help him through this ordeal.

She sat in the back seat of the squad for what seemed like hours. The rain tapered off, becoming a light drizzle. Officer Finley finally returned, sliding behind the wheel.

"I'll take you back to our precinct for your statement," he said as he started the engine. "When we're finished, I'll take you home."

For a moment, the small yet cozy house in Dalton, Georgia, that she'd shared with her mother and sister flashed in her mind. An intense longing hit hard. She desperately wished they could go back to the way things were. To the time of her life before her mother died. Before Kate had disappeared.

To the career she'd once loved.

Now her mother was gone, her sister was missing, and her home was a dingy motel room.

Tears pricked at her eyes. *Stop it*, she told herself sternly. No sense in focusing on what she'd lost. Her priority was to find Kate and from there to move forward with supporting her sister. She shook off the flash of self-pity and met the officer's gaze in the rearview mirror. "Thanks. Will Officer Murphy be there too?"

Finley hesitated. "He'll be giving his statement to another officer."

She figured that meant she and Sawyer wouldn't be able to talk to each other. It was understandable that the police would want to hear both of their stories separately, for accuracy and to prevent any sort of collusion.

But knowing she couldn't see him sent a fluttering of panic coursing through her. And it only reinforced how accustomed she'd gotten to having Sawyer's support.

For the first time, she wondered what her life would be like after finding Kate and returning to Dalton.

One thing was for certain, there would be a gaping hole in her heart when she was forced to leave Chattanooga and Sawyer Murphy behind.

SAWYER SAT CALMLY in the interrogation room of the precinct located near East Ridge, his sopping wet clothes sticking uncomfortably to his skin. He knew the drill and had been on the other side of the interrogation more than once.

He reiterated how the events had unfolded resulting in his fatally shooting Melvin Curtis. He answered every single question they asked, even when they were the same questions over and over again.

The only part of this process that worried him was how Naomi was holding up. She wasn't accustomed to this sort of thing, and he could see her losing her patience with the repetitive and tedious process.

It was still incredulous to him that she'd escaped Melvin's grip in the first place. The officer kept pressing him on that issue, and Sawyer had repeatedly told him he didn't have any clue how she'd accomplished that feat. All he could say for certain was that he saw the muzzle of Melvin's gun turning toward her, an act that caused him to fire twice to save her.

After what felt like an eternity, the officers finally left him alone. Sawyer knew full well someone was likely watching him on camera or through the one-way mirror, so he didn't let his facial expression change. However, he did wring out his clothing the best he could, making small puddles of water on the floor.

When the door opened revealing his boss, Lieutenant Watkins, he inwardly groaned as he rose to his feet. "Lieutenant."

"Murphy." His boss eyed him warily for a moment before gesturing to the chair. "Sit down. Why hasn't anyone brought you dry clothes?"

He suspected it was because they wanted him to remain uncomfortable and off balance, hoping he'd mess up his story. He shrugged. "It doesn't matter."

Watkins grimaced, then leaned forward putting his elbows on the table. "Murphy, didn't I warn you about letting this get too personal?"

"Yes, sir. But that's not why I fired at Curtis. He ignored my demand to drop his weapon and turned to shoot Ms. Palmer. I had no choice but to take action."

"We don't even know Curtis is involved in the missing girls," his boss said sharply. "And now we never will."

Sawyer desperately wished things had gone down differently. He'd wanted to take Curtis alive, to get him to tell him where Louisa and Kate were being held. It burned to know the man's secrets had died with him.

Yet he hadn't been willing to sacrifice Naomi's life to get the information either. And there was nothing he could do to change what had happened. "His dying is regrettable. But I don't see how I could have avoided shooting him."

"Are you sure about that?" His lieutenant's gaze was skeptical. "You may have overreacted to Ms. Palmer being in danger."

He did his best to ignore the flicker of anger. Drawing

every ounce of self-control he possessed, he repeated his statement for the millionth time. "Curtis refused to drop his weapon. When Ms. Palmer broke free of his grasp, the muzzle of his gun swung toward her. Believing he intended to shoot her, I fired twice, aiming at center mass and hitting him in the chest as we are trained to do."

Watkins sat back and crossed his arms over his chest. "That's your story."

"That's the truth. Sir." He met his boss's gaze head-on.

A heavy silence fell between them. Finally, his lieutenant pushed away from the table and stood. "You'll be on paid leave until you're cleared by IAB."

"Yes, sir." His gut clenched at hearing the dreaded initials referencing the internal affairs bureau, but he tried not to show his reaction. Watkins was following formal protocol, so he couldn't blame him. "Uh, sir?"

The lieutenant paused at the door. "What?"

Sawyer tried to choose his words carefully. "I don't believe Detective Turner has had a chance to interview Ms. Palmer about her missing sister and the possible connection to Louisa Marchese's disappearance."

His boss's gaze bored into his, likely reading between the lines that Sawyer didn't think Turner was doing a good enough job on the case. The lieutenant finally spoke. "I'll request an updated report from Detective Turner in the morning."

Sawyer nodded, knowing his boss wasn't going to share anything more. Turner wouldn't be happy, but Sawyer didn't care.

Although he wished he knew what the unknown female's cause of death was. Could he make a quick call to the ME's office before they learned he was on paid leave?

"I'd like to use the restroom," he said loudly.

The door opened a minute later. "Officer Murphy, you're free to go. But we respectfully request you stay in the area until the investigation is complete."

"I understand." He left the interview room, pulling his phone from his pocket. Thankfully, he used a waterproof case, or he doubted the stupid thing would work.

Outside the station, he swept his gaze over the area, searching for Naomi. He tried not to panic when he couldn't find any sign of her. He called her cell phone, relieved when she answered.

"Sawyer? Are you okay?"

Her concern for him was heartwarming. It had been a long time since a woman had been worried about him. "I'm fine, where are you?"

"Officer Finley drove me back to the motel."

"Okay, that's good." No one had bothered to offer him a ride, but hopefully his SUV was still at the gas station. He didn't see any reason why it would be considered part of the crime scene. "I'll be there as soon as I can."

"Okay. I'm glad you've been released."

"Take care and don't open the door to anyone," he cautioned.

"I won't."

He disconnected from the call and then dialed the ME's office. It was late, but thankfully someone answered.

"This is Officer Murphy with the Chattanooga PD. I'm wondering if the ME has identified a cause of death on the unknown female found outside of East Ridge."

"It will take time for the toxicology results to come in, but the initial cause of death is blunt force trauma to the back of the head."

Interesting. A blow to the back of the head could indicate the victim was running away from her attacker.

Although the body still could have been dumped there if the escape had taken place elsewhere. "Okay, thank you."

Tucking his phone back into his water-laden jeans pocket, he turned and headed back inside. The least his fellow officers could do was give him a lift back to his car.

One of the two officers who'd interrogated him for the past several hours grudgingly agreed to take him to the gas station.

"Thanks." Sawyer got out of the squad, gazing over to where a group of officers were still processing the crime scene. He wanted to look around for himself, see if he could find the infamous black Buick, but he knew he'd only get into trouble with his boss.

Now he knew how helpless it felt to be the family member of a victim. To sit back and wait to hear what if anything came out of a police investigation.

It was super frustrating to be left out of the communication loop.

After sliding in behind the wheel of his SUV, Sawyer turned around and headed back to downtown Chattanooga and the motel where he'd secured a room next to Naomi's.

He showered and changed into his uniform, which was his only dry clothing, before knocking lightly at Naomi's door.

"Sawyer." Stark relief was etched on her features. She opened the door wider, wordlessly inviting him inside. She'd showered and changed too, her hair soft around her face. "Why on earth did they keep you so long?"

He shrugged, downplaying the endless interrogation. "They wanted to be sure my story was accurate."

"You're a police officer just like they are." She looked troubled. "I don't understand why they wouldn't believe you."

"A man is dead." The words came out sharper than he intended. He sighed and softened his tone. "It's their job to prove my shooting him was justified."

"It's my fault," Naomi said in a low voice. She sank down onto the edge of the bed. "I shouldn't have let him grab me."

Sawyer dropped into a chair across from her. "I'm curious as to what happened. Did Curtis get to you inside the store?"

"Yes. The restrooms were located way in the back. There was an exit nearby, so when I came out of the restroom, he grabbed my arm and pressed a gun into my side. Before I could blink, he'd pushed me through the exit along the very back of the building."

It was all too easy to imagine the chain of events. "I'm sorry you had to go through that," Sawyer murmured. "But I don't understand how he knew you were there in the first place."

"I don't know, and Officer Finley asked me the same thing. I don't remember seeing him when I went inside." She frowned. "And I don't think he could have followed us."

Sawyer had chosen to use his SUV specifically to avoid that scenario. Although maybe Curtis had been hanging around the crime scene where they'd found the dead girl. Some perps got off on that. He focused on Naomi. "I knew something was wrong when you called me."

The corner of her mouth lifted in a halfhearted smile. "And I knew you'd understand something was wrong if I didn't answer."

He reached over to take her hand in his. "I lost several years of my life believing he was going to kill you."

All hints of a smile faded from her features. "I feel

awful you had to shoot him, Sawyer. That couldn't have been easy."

"It was the first time I've been forced to shoot a man while being a law enforcement officer." The admission slipped out before he could stop it.

"I was afraid of that." Naomi came up off the bed and knelt beside him. "I'm so thankful you saved me, Sawyer. But I wish it hadn't been necessary."

He didn't deserve her sympathy. Her kindness. But he didn't have the willpower to push her away either. "I told him to drop his weapon."

"Yes, you did, more than once. And he didn't obey. Not even when he was lying on the ground, bleeding." She cupped his face in her hand. "I know in my heart God sent you to protect me, Sawyer. I will forever be in your debt."

A lump filled in the back of his throat, making it impossible for him to speak. Her kindness floored him, but she didn't know the truth.

That Melvin Curtis wasn't the first man he'd killed.

And deep down, he couldn't believe God had forgiven him for what he'd done the evening the cabin had started on fire thirteen years ago.

CHAPTER THIRTEEN

"Please don't feel guilty for what happened." Naomi held Sawyer's gaze, silently pleading with him. "You're a good man."

"Not that good." The hint of bitterness caught her off guard.

"You are." She really didn't understand why he didn't seem to believe in himself.

He blew out a heavy sigh and shook his head. "You don't know what happened that night."

She froze. "What night?"

"The night of the fire." He grimaced. "It's my fault the Preacher and his wife died that night."

She did her best not to show any reaction. "What do you mean? I can't imagine you'd start a fire on purpose."

"No, not the fire." He hesitated, then blurted out, "I poisoned their food."

The news shocked her. "What?"

He swallowed hard. "Exactly what I said. I poisoned him and Ruth, using pokeweed berries."

Her heart squeezed in her chest. "Oh, Sawyer, I'm so

sorry. You mentioned abuse, but it must have been worse than I imagined. I'm sure you must have been desperate to escape."

He let out a harsh sound. "Yeah, you could say that. The Preacher ranted and raved at us, hit us with a switch as he preached about the fires of hell and how we were such awful sinners. He also made us sleep in the cellar, which is why I reveled in working the garden." He hesitated, then added, "I was fourteen when we finally managed to escape."

"Oh, Sawyer." Her heart broke for him.

"Don't you see? If I hadn't mixed those poisonous berries in with the blueberries Ruth made into a pie, they'd both still be alive."

"You don't know that." She took his hand in hers. "He may have died in the fire regardless."

"No, all seven of us managed to escape, I'm sure they could have too. If I hadn't poisoned them."

Sawyer's guilt-ridden expression tore at her heart. "Sawyer, that man tortured you and the other foster kids while his wife did nothing to stop it. You were young, I'm sure your intent was only to escape, nothing more."

"Yeah, but in law enforcement, we call that manslaughter in the first degree." Sawyer drew his hand from hers. "I performed an act that I should have reasonably known could have caused his death."

She didn't know what to say or what to do to help him. "Sawyer, you couldn't have reasonably expected a fire to break out in the cabin on the same night he ate some poisonous berries baked into a pie. You need to understand this may have been God's way of helping you and the other kids escape an impossible situation."

Sawyer gently pushed her away and rose to his feet.

"You honestly don't think I'm responsible for the Preacher's and his wife's deaths?"

"You're not responsible for the fire." She stood to face him. "And really, how many of those berries could he have eaten?"

For a moment, Sawyer looked uncertain. "I don't know. They're extremely bitter, so I made sure to mix them in with blueberries and of course sugar to mask the taste. I worried he or Ruth would figure it out, but they didn't. None of us kids were impacted because they never gave us dessert. That special treat was only for the two of them, especially the Preacher."

"So that means the man who physically and emotionally abused you, kept you and the other kids locked in a cellar, may have simply gotten sick." She desperately wanted Sawyer to realize he wasn't responsible for the Preacher's and his wife's deaths.

"Maybe. But the end result was that they died in the fire, probably because they were too sick to escape the cabin."

"You don't know that for sure, Sawyer." She tipped her head to the side. "How did the fire start anyway?"

He slowly shook his head. "I don't know. We all scattered in the woods afterward, there wasn't time to compare notes. I figured a log from the fire rolled out into the cabin and they were too sick to notice."

"You had nothing to do with the fire," she pressed.

"No. Hailey woke me up saying she smelled smoke. I remember we woke up the rest of the kids and headed up the stairs to the main cabin."

"The door wasn't locked?"

He frowned. "No, I don't think so. Jayme was there, helping to pull us out of the cellar. It's all a little hazy. The place was already engulfed in flames, and we were all so terrified. We barely made it out alive."

She reached over and gripped his hand. "Sawyer, if the fact that you got out alive is partially because the Preacher and his wife were sick in bed, then I'm glad. Very glad you and the others didn't die that night."

"But . . ." His voice trailed off.

"God helps those who help themselves, remember?" She stepped closer so that she could put her arms around his waist. "You only wanted to escape, Sawyer. No one would ever blame you for that."

"I'm—not sure that's true."

"It's true." She tightened her grip. "Think about it from a cop's perspective. If you had come upon a fire in a cabin, with seven foster kids hiding in the woods, one of them only fourteen, explaining the horror they'd lived in, wouldn't you believe their actions to be self-defense?"

"There has to be an imminent threat of harm to count as self-defense."

"You were kids, Sawyer. Doing your best to survive a horrible situation." She tightened her grip around his waist. "Please consider the idea that God was watching over you that night. That God wanted you and the others to escape."

"I want to believe that." His voice was so soft she could barely hear it.

"Trust me, Sawyer." She went up on her tippy toes and kissed him. Her goal was to offer comfort and support, but in a nanosecond, heat flared between them.

Sawyer deepened their kiss as if he needed her to survive.

As she needed him. Her head spun from the impact of their embrace. She clung to his broad shoulders, secretly thrilled when he gathered her closer still. Sawyer's embrace was so different from Tony's. Sawyer made her feel desired yet safe at the same time. She had the sense he'd never pressure her for more than she was ready to give.

Sawyer broke off from their kiss but still cradled her close. It took a few moments for her to gather her scattered thoughts.

"I—um, you—um, need to get some sleep." Sawyer's husky voice sent a shiver of awareness down her spine. She tightened her grip momentarily, before reluctantly letting him go.

"I—yes. You're probably right." She stared up at him for a long minute. "You're a very special person, Sawyer. I want you to know that."

He shook his head, a bemused expression crossing his face. "I haven't told anyone about that night. Never told a soul about how I mixed pokeweed berries in a pie that was eaten by the Preacher and his wife. I thought you'd go running off in the opposite direction."

Her heart melted. "Never. Thanks for trusting me with your secret. And know that no matter what, God is always there for us. For you."

He nodded and moved toward the door.

"Sawyer?"

He paused and glanced over his shoulder.

"Thank you for saving my life tonight."

"You helped."

"I hate knowing you might be in trouble because of me."

"I'm not." He paused, then added, "But I'm officially on paid leave, pending the outcome of the investigation."

The implication of that hit hard. Not just the impact to Sawyer's career, which was bad enough, but how would they find Kate now?

"I guess Melvin Curtis was our best lead in finding

Kate." She put a hand on the doorjamb to steady herself. "I'm not sure where to look next."

"Get some sleep." Sawyer gave her a reassuring smile. "We'll talk about next steps in the morning."

"Okay." She forced a smile. "Good night, Sawyer."

"Good night." He disappeared through the doorway. She shot the dead bolt home, then added the chain latch as well. With Melvin's death, the only person who could still come after her was leering man. And so far, the sketch she'd helped create hadn't provided any results.

For all she knew, leering man had gotten far away from Chattanooga. He could even be in another state by this time. And if that was the case, she feared they'd never find Kate.

Never.

SAWYER COULDN'T BELIEVE he'd spilled his guts to Naomi about that night thirteen years ago.

And that her response to the news of what he'd done hadn't been to look at him with disgust or run away screaming.

Oh no, her response had been to kiss him.

She'd kissed him!

And what had he done? He'd grabbed her close and kissed her back as if he couldn't live another day without her. What was he thinking? Honestly, he hadn't been thinking at all, which was the problem.

Thankfully, she hadn't slapped him. Or seemed to be the least bit upset. In fact, she'd continued holding on to him as if she may have been knocked off balance by the power of their kiss the same way he'd been.

He still wasn't sure how he'd found the strength to walk away. Especially when all he'd really wanted to do was kiss her again.

Shaking his head at his foolishness, he washed up and crawled into bed. Gazing up at the ceiling, he thought again about her response to his telling her his darkest secret.

He'd thought he'd still feel guilty, but after baring his soul, he felt relieved. Lighter. Maybe simply sharing his burden had helped relieve the pressure he'd kept buried deep inside.

Was she right about God? All this time, he'd battled guilt over killing the Preacher and his wife when the fire had been the real culprit.

He hadn't started the fire and didn't think any of the foster kids had. Not even Jayme, although he never did figure out how she'd helped them get out of the cellar. He'd asked, but she'd claimed the cellar door wasn't locked.

And maybe it wasn't. He'd often wondered if the Preacher was so sick from the pokeweed berries that he'd forgotten to lock it. The same way he hadn't noticed a log rolling out of the fireplace.

Whatever. That part didn't really matter. But now that Sawyer really thought back to that night, he realized there may have been some truth to what Naomi had said.

One slice of blueberry mixed with pokeweed berry pie may not have been enough to kill either of them. Make them sick to their stomach, yeah. But then the fire had happened, and they'd all escaped without any sign of the Preacher or his wife getting outside the cabin that night.

When the police and firetrucks had arrived, they'd split up and melted into the woods, getting as far away from the place as they could manage.

So far, Hailey Donovan was the only foster he knew that had survived and thrived. Cooper and Trent had gone off on their own shortly before he'd been caught stealing by Officer Kohl. Joe had taken him in, had given him a roof over his head, food in his belly, and had basically saved his life.

Sawyer and Joe had tried to find Cooper and Trent, but without success. And he felt a little guilty about that too. Not because he hadn't been able to find them, they'd all learned how to disappear.

But because he'd failed to keep the three of them together. Sawyer knew with every fiber of his being that if Joe Kohl had found all three of them, the cop would have supported all of them, keeping them together.

Sawyer was a cop today only because of what Joe had done for him. Joe had not just provided shelter, but he had enrolled him in school and encouraged him to take the police academy exam when he graduated.

All because Joe claimed to see a bit of himself in Sawyer.

He owed his life to Joe, and when the man had died two years ago from a sudden heart attack, he'd lost the only father figure he'd ever known.

Sawyer had vague and not very good memories of his mother. Looking back, he knew she'd tried her best to provide him with food and shelter, but based on the numerous male visitors that had been in and out of their place, he suspected she'd been working as a prostitute.

He'd been removed from her custody when he was seven. Had been sent to a variety of foster homes until landing with the Preacher shortly after his ninth birthday.

Sawyer tried to push the old memories aside. And must have fallen asleep at some point because the next thing he knew, light was streaming in through the motel room window.

He showered and dressed again in his uniform, although he'd need different clothes to wear, and soon, since he was officially on paid leave. Being caught in uniform could cause him to be suspended without pay.

After making a cup of coffee, he heard noise from Naomi's room. Sipping from his cup, he went outside and lightly rapped on her door.

"Hi, Sawyer," she greeted him with a warm smile. "Come on in."

He crossed the threshold and closed the door behind him.

"I was hoping we could head over to the restaurant for breakfast, if you're hungry." Naomi glanced at him as she set her bag of personal items on the bed.

"I'd love breakfast, but I need to return home for a change of clothing first." He gestured to his uniform. "Can't risk being seen in this while on leave of absence. It's against the rules."

She grimaced. "We don't want that. Would you mind if I rode with you?"

He offered a lopsided smile. "I was hoping you would. I know I'm off duty, but I'll still feel better once leering guy is in custody."

"Me too." A shadow crossed her features. "Soon, right?"

"Yeah." He didn't voice his concern that if leering man knew about Curtis being killed, he'd stay well-hidden or disappear from Chattanooga once and for all.

Unless there was a really good reason for him to stick around. Like maybe the sex-trafficking ring still had girls hidden nearby.

Had he and Naomi gotten too close in East Ridge? Was that why Curtis had grabbed her?

The only way to know for sure was to head back to that area to poke around a bit. Although he couldn't afford to be seen anywhere near the crime scene where he'd shot Curtis.

Finding leering man was important, but he didn't want to lose his job. Especially since the Chattanooga police were searching for leering man too.

He shook off the troubled thoughts. "If you're ready, let's go."

"I'm ready." Naomi reached for her bag, but he took it from her. He noticed she'd helped herself to the motel room coffee too.

"We can grab a fast-food breakfast sandwich along the way," he offered, carrying her bag out to his SUV.

"That would be great." She slid into the passenger seat.

He kept a sharp eye out for anything suspicious as he left the motel and headed to his cabin. Curtis was no longer a threat, but he couldn't say for sure if Melvin Curtis was the one who'd come to his cabin that night or if it was leering guy.

It pained him to realize he couldn't necessarily keep Naomi with him at the cabin. They'd have to find yet another motel room.

In East Ridge? If he was alone, he wouldn't hesitate. But with Naomi he couldn't take the risk.

They stopped for bacon and egg sandwiches along with more coffee before heading out of town. There wasn't much traffic on the highway leading to his place, although the early morning mist did cause him to drive much slower than usual. It was close to eight o'clock in the morning when he finally pulled into his long, winding driveway.

"Stay in the car for a few minutes." Sawyer slid out from

behind the wheel and did a quick sweep around his cabin. His trip lines were still in place, which was somewhat reassuring. Next, he went inside the cabin to make sure there was no one hiding inside, before returning to his SUV. "It's all clear."

"Thanks." Naomi jumped down and followed him inside. He wished he had a large guard dog, but of course, it was too late for that.

He'd always wanted a dog. Joe had been allergic, and in the two years since the man he'd loved as a father had been gone, Sawyer had been too busy with his career to get one from the local shelter.

Did Naomi like dogs? And why did he care if she did? It wasn't as if they would be seeing each other once this was over. He didn't do the house in the suburbs thing, with neighborhood parties, remember?

The thought was depressing.

"Make yourself at home. I'll be back soon." He disappeared into his room and quickly changed.

He'd been forced to hand over his service weapon and his badge. But Sawyer had a personal weapon, too, along with the proper permit to carry it.

He clipped the small gun into an ankle holster, hoping and praying he wouldn't have to use it.

When he returned to the living room, he found Naomi on the phone. She turned to face him.

"Yes, Detective, I can come in to talk in about thirty minutes. Thanks for calling."

"Detective Turner finally reached out to you?" Sawyer asked, trying not to show his annoyance.

"Yes." She grimaced. "I hate to ask you for more favors, but I'll need a ride back to the precinct."

"I don't mind, after all, I'm the one who pointed out to

my boss that Turner hadn't had a chance to talk to you in the first place."

"You didn't have to do that," she protested.

"Yeah, I did." Sawyer waved a hand. "I don't mind driving you back, Naomi. It's about time Turner stepped up his investigation. The man is slower than molasses. You were kidnapped, and your sister is missing, just like Louisa. There must be some similarities between the two cases."

"I wish you could sit through the interview with me," she said as they headed back outside.

Personally, Sawyer wished the same thing. Although he'd already heard her story, while Turner hadn't, except secondhand from him.

"Don't worry, I'll wait for you outside, okay? You'll be safe enough inside the police station."

She was silent for a moment as they settled into his SUV. He turned it around to head out onto the highway. "It's not that, Sawyer. You're the one who has been there for me from the very beginning. I trust you."

Hearing that was humbling. "Naomi, you're a strong woman and a survivor. You've escaped your kidnappers and Melvin Curtis. I am glad to be here with you but don't sell yourself short." He glanced over, then took her small hand in his. "You'll be fine."

Tightly gripping his hand, she nodded. "I know, but I wouldn't be here without you."

He belatedly realized that Naomi might be experiencing a bit of survivor's guilt. That maybe she hadn't kissed him because she cared about him on a personal level. But because she saw him as some sort of hero. Despite the way he'd confessed to poisoning the Preacher.

All the more reason to put some distance between them.

To make sure she understood their relationship was that of two friends helping each other out.

That she didn't owe him anything.

The loud crack of gunfire interrupted his thoughts. "Get down," he shouted, hitting the gas and barreling down the highway in an effort to escape the shooter.

CHAPTER FOURTEEN

More gunfire? Why? Naomi bent over so her head was down between her knees, her temples pounding with pain while her mind spun in circles at the knowledge that they were once again being targeted.

And since Melvin Curtis was dead, that left leering man as the shooter.

Straining to listen, she was relieved not to hear additional gunfire. She hesitantly sat up, glancing around at the vehicle.

"We're not hit?"

Sawyer's expression was grim. "No, although that was far too close to my cabin for comfort. We're only two miles from the place."

She couldn't disagree and laced her shaking fingers together in an effort to remain calm. "But if they knew we were at your cabin, I don't understand why they waited until we were leaving to shoot."

He shot her a glance. "You make a very good point. I'll report the gunfire when we get to the station, but it's clear the cabin has been compromised."

She swallowed hard, feeling terrible about bringing Sawyer into the mess that was her life. "I'm sorry."

"You didn't take the shot," Sawyer said evenly. "And I probably shouldn't have risked going back, not after I knew an intruder had been on my property."

"I'm sure you thought it was Melvin Curtis. Only now we know it must be leering man." She shook her head. "Why he's hanging around is a mystery."

"Yes, it is." Sawyer frowned. "I feel like we're missing something. These two guys aren't acting like your typical sex traffickers."

"Is there really a typical person who does that?" She shivered in spite of the warmth. "What a horrible thought."

"Sex traffickers are all about getting girls to work for money. They don't care about killing people, the way Curtis and leering man seem to be focusing on. Normally, they would simply take the girls and go to a new place. Unfortunately, there is no limit as to where they can go to start up a new business."

She grimaced, feeling sick at the idea Kate was in this kind of trouble. "It's terrible."

"Yes, it is." Sawyer's low voice was full of agony. "And I'd do anything to stop it."

She reached over to rest her hand on his arm. "I'm touched you care so much."

He looked surprised. "Why wouldn't I?"

"I don't know, it just seems that a lot of people haven't made breaking up these rings a priority. Otherwise, why would these girls keep disappearing?"

Sawyer was silent for a moment. "I'm not so sure it's lack of caring, but lack of resources. Murder and other violent crimes tend to be the top priority. And unfortunately, there's no shortage of that to go around."

"I know. I used to be an ICU nurse, remember? We saw evidence of violent crime all the time."

"I'm sure you did," Sawyer agreed.

She gazed out the window as they headed into town. Despite the violence she'd experienced here, she found she liked the city of Chattanooga. It wasn't that much bigger than Dalton, and the backdrop of the Smoky Mountains created a strange sense of isolation intermingled with peace.

Or maybe she was romanticizing the place because of Sawyer. With his dark hair and intense dark eyes, he was far more handsome than Tony Baldwin. A much nicer guy, one who seemed to truly care about others.

Satisfied with his job at the carpet factory, Tony only wanted to have a good time.

Naomi knew now she didn't care about Tony as much as she should care about a man she was dating. But that didn't mean Sawyer was interested in stepping into a relationship.

She pushed away the thought. Ridiculous to think about dating a guy when her sister was missing. Finding Kate was the reason she'd come here.

She closed her eyes and bowed her head. *God, please keep Kate safe in Your care.*

"Naomi?" She lifted her head when Sawyer touched her arm. "Are you okay?"

"Fine." She belatedly realized he'd pulled into the parking lot of the precinct. "I'm ready."

"You'll do great."

She jumped out of the car, glancing along the passenger side to check for evidence of gunfire. But she didn't see anything. "Are you still planning to report the gunfire to your boss?"

"Yeah." Sawyer shrugged. "I almost wish he'd hit the

vehicle so I'd have proof, other than just my word."

"Your word as a cop should be more than enough." She was getting perturbed with the local police. It seemed as if they weren't taking these threats seriously.

"I'm sure it will be," Sawyer said, although she still didn't believe him.

She headed inside and told the clerk behind the glass that she was here to talk to Detective Turner.

"Oh yes, he's expecting you. This way please." The male officer opened a door for her. She followed him down a short hall to a small interview room. "Have a seat, Detective Turner will be here shortly."

"Thanks." She sat and laced her fingers together in her lap. There was no reason to be nervous, yet she couldn't seem to quell her nerves.

Turner made her wait a full ten minutes before joining her. So much for expecting her.

"Ms. Palmer, I'm Detective Turner."

She gave a curt nod. He was older than she'd expected, maybe early forties. His dark hair was turning gray around his temples.

"Okay, let's see." He sat across from her with a pad of paper. "Why don't you start at the beginning?"

His rather blunt, matter-of-fact attitude wasn't reassuring. She explained about how her sister hadn't come home from work and that a friend had noticed Kate getting a ride in a boxy white van. Then she went on about how she'd followed the white boxy van from Dalton across the Tennessee border, been rear-ended, then kidnapped. She paused, expecting him to ask questions, but he simply regarded her steadily.

"Go on," he encouraged.

He hadn't written anything down, which irked her. She

went on to describe how she'd escaped the kidnappers, hid in the woods, and was picked up a while later by Officer Murphy.

"Then what? Where did Officer Murphy take you?"

The detective's question raised the tiny hairs on the back of her neck. Was he looking for a way to harm Sawyer's reputation? Were there bad feelings between the two men?

"He offered to take me to a motel." That much was true. She didn't want to lie, but she wasn't about to throw Sawyer under the bus either. "Can we get back to my sister, Kate, for a moment? She's sixteen and has been missing for three, no four days now. Do you know if anyone else has seen a boxy white van around here?"

Turner hesitated, then said, "Not to my knowledge. You didn't get a license plate number?"

"No. It was dark, and I was staying back, hoping they wouldn't notice me following them. But they must have, otherwise why would they bother to run me off the road and kidnap me?"

"It could be a coincidence. You're a pretty woman, and some men have no scruples."

It wasn't easy to hold herself back. "No, it's more than that. And it's not a coincidence. They knew I was searching for my sister."

"They said that?" Turner looked surprised.

"Not directly, no." She thought back to those frightening moments she'd been stuck with Curtis and leering man. "I asked several times where they were taking me, and leering man told me I'd find out soon enough. Oh, and the leering man told the driver to keep an eye out for the road. Sawyer found a dirt road that stopped a few yards in from the highway."

"Hmm." Turner stared down at his notepad for a moment. "I called the Dalton police, they seem to believe your sister ran away."

She felt her cheeks flush. "She didn't. I'm telling you, she was taken away in that boxy white van."

"There isn't any proof of that."

"Isn't it your job to find that proof?" She held on to her temper with an effort. "I'm telling you my sister was kidnapped. And I hear there's a young girl by the name of Louisa missing here too. A dead girl was found in the brush, and Melvin Curtis who was one of the kidnappers tried to kill me. Why aren't you trying to find out if there are similarities between the three cases?"

"I'm the detective here, you aren't." He wrote something on his notepad that looked like the word runaway. "I'm looking into all angles of these cases, down to the last detail."

"You could have fooled me." Naomi jumped to her feet. "Whatever. I'm done talking to you."

He shot to his feet. "You can't leave until we're finished."

Fear curled through her, but she lifted her chin and looked him in the eye. "I came here voluntarily. You can't hold me against my will."

Turner stared at her, but a knock at the door distracted him. The door opened, and the lieutenant Sawyer had introduced her to yesterday stood there. "Is there a problem?"

"No, Lieutenant." Turner stepped aside. "Ms. Palmer doesn't have any more information for us. She's ready to leave."

The lieutenant looked at her, then opened the door wider. "Of course. Thanks for coming in, Ms. Palmer."

"Yeah, well, you can thank me by finding my sister. And if you ask me, that guy"—she jabbed her thumb at Turner—"isn't doing enough."

The lieutenant frowned but didn't say anything more. Any hope she'd harbored about Detective Turner actually finding her sister vanished.

Unable to hide her disgust at how her interview had gone, she walked through the police station and into the early morning sun. She stopped and lifted her face to the warmth, determined to release her anger.

Being upset with Turner wouldn't help find Kate. At least she had support from Sawyer. Even if he was officially on leave of absence.

"Naomi?" Sawyer's low husky voice had her turning to face him. "How did it go?"

She tried to smile. "He's utterly useless if you ask me. But I did my duty by telling him what I know."

"I'm sorry." Sawyer came over and opened the passenger door for her.

"Did your boss believe you about the gunfire?"

"Yeah, I think he did." Sawyer looked somewhat relieved as he said this.

"Good." At least one thing went right for them. She slid into the SUV and closed the door. Now they needed to find leering man, before he took another shot at them.

As far as she could tell, leering man was their only lead to finding Kate.

SAWYER WASN'T happy that Naomi's interview with Turner hadn't gone well, but he'd done what he could in letting the lieutenant know his opinion. His boss mentioned he'd insisted the FBI get involved, which would help immensely. Sawyer let the lieutenant know Naomi would gladly talk to the Feds. He felt bad he hadn't followed through with taking her to their office, but things had been a bit hairy over the past few days.

His boss had gotten upset when Sawyer had explained about the gunfire. The lieutenant didn't take shooting at a cop lightly, and for a moment, Sawyer thought his boss would put him back on active duty.

But he didn't. After telling Sawyer to be careful, his boss had promised to keep him updated on the investigation related to the shooting of Melvin Curtis and the identity of the unknown female, for which Sawyer was grateful.

"We need to find a place to stay for at least the next twenty-four hours." He backed the SUV out of the parking space.

"How about one in East Ridge?"

Shocked, he glanced at her. "Are you crazy? You were almost killed in East Ridge."

"I know, Sawyer. But don't you think that's the most logical place to find leering man?"

Yeah, he did. Had thought the same thing about staying there. "It's too dangerous."

"We're already in danger. They found us outside your place, remember?" Naomi said stubbornly.

He couldn't deny it made sense to go on offense rather than running from this guy. It would be an easy decision to make if not for the small problem of putting Naomi in danger.

As if reading his thoughts, she lightly grasped his arm. "Kate is my sister. I need to find her. Detective Turner isn't going to do diddly squat. Please, Sawyer, you're the only one who can help me."

He didn't want to admit she was right. Turner was mired so deep in ridiculous details Sawyer didn't think he'd ever find a connection between the dead girl, Kate, and Louisa. If there was one.

The ME's office had deemed the unknown female's cause of death to be blunt force trauma to the head. Which was interesting as it leaned more toward the girl running from her assailant and being hit on the back of the head. It was a grim yet highly probable scenario.

"Sawyer? Please?" Naomi repeated in a pleading tone.

She was difficult to resist. "Okay, we'll see if we can find a motel near East Ridge."

"In the city would be better." She released his arm, and oddly, he missed her touch. "We need to find leering man before he hurts someone else."

Sawyer didn't like knowing she was right about the need to find leering man. Had the girl in the woods been murdered by Curtis or the leering man?

Or someone else?

"Do me a favor," he said as he drove toward East Ridge. "We're almost at the city limits. I need you to keep your head down until I can find us a place to stay."

She wrinkled her nose but did as he asked, tucking her head down near her feet. "This makes my head throb, and you should be glad I don't experience motion sickness or doing this would probably make me puke," she said in a muffled voice. "Especially earlier when you were pretending to be an Indy 500 race car driver."

Her teasing comment made him smile. Trust Naomi to try to lighten a grim situation.

"I'm sorry it makes your head hurt." He raked his gaze over the city, trying to remember where the reasonably priced motels were located. He was hoping for something low budget so they could use cash without being hassled for a credit card.

Using a card was fine under normal circumstances, but these were anything but. He had no way of knowing which motel owners or their respective employees were working with those involved in sex trafficking.

And he didn't want to find out the hard way by trusting the wrong person.

Cruising past the gas station near Melvin Curtis's crime scene, he could see the area had finally been cleared of all yellow tape and police personnel. He found himself sending up a silent prayer that he'd be cleared of any wrongdoing.

He wasn't sure why his go-to response was to reach out to a God he didn't entirely believe in. Naomi's influence? Maybe.

A low-budget motel caught his eye. Warily, he drove past it, glancing at his rearview mirror.

No sign of a tail since leaving the police station. But he decided to drive around a bit before heading back to the motel.

"Are we there yet?" Naomi asked.

"Soon," he promised, taking another turn. "The motel I'm considering happens to be located less than a mile from the gas station where Melvin grabbed you."

"That sounds perfect," Naomi said.

He shook his head. "Only you would think so. It's a two-star motel, a ranking obviously designated by someone feeling generous."

"Hey, it's better than sleeping in the woods," she shot back.

"Yeah." Considering how many nights he'd slept in the woods, he had to agree. After escaping the Preacher and spending years in the cellar, he and the others had preferred living outdoors. He'd raided the garden before disappearing from the cabin and had learned enough to survive over those next few weeks.

Eventually, being rained on got old and they were forced to seek shelter in places much like the one he was heading toward. But even then he'd only been able to sleep with a window open, no matter how hot or cold the outside temperature might be.

"Sawyer? My head is hurting from being bent over like this."

Naomi brought him back to the present. "Almost there." He turned into the parking lot, then drove behind the corner of the building where his SUV couldn't be seen from the road.

"Can I sit up now?" Naomi asked when the SUV came to a stop.

"Yes." He glanced at her. "Sorry about that, but I needed to be sure we weren't followed."

"I know." She pushed her hair from her face. "This place doesn't look too bad."

"We haven't seen the inside of the rooms yet." He hesitated, then asked, "Do you trust me?"

"What? Yes, of course I trust you."

He drew in a deep breath. "Getting connecting rooms might raise suspicions. I'd like to get one room with two double beds." He turned to face her. "I promise you don't have any reason to be afraid I'll take advantage of you."

She blushed and waved a hand. "I'm not worried. You're not like that, Sawyer."

Her trust was humbling. "Thanks. This way I'll be a single guy getting one room. No one has to know you'll be staying there with me."

"It's okay," she repeated. "I'm fine."

He tossed her the key fob and slid out from behind the wheel. "If anything happens, I want you to drive back to the police station. The lieutenant will listen to you."

"Okay." A hint of fear shadowed her blue eyes.

He smiled reassuringly, then slammed the door. He walked around the corner toward the front of the building. There was a small lobby with a neon red vacancy sign in the window.

A man emerged from a room, letting the door shut loudly behind him. Moving instinctively, Sawyer hugged the wall, making himself small as he watched the man stride toward the lobby. Something about him was familiar. The image of Naomi's sketch flashed in his mind.

Leering man?

No, it couldn't be. What were the chances they'd end up at the same motel as Naomi's leering guy?

He needed to get a better look at the guy's face. Sawyer was glad he was casually dressed in black jeans and a black T-shirt. And that he still had the small gun in his ankle holster.

Easing forward, he abruptly stopped when the lobby door opened and the same guy emerged.

Now that he could see his face, the resemblance was clear. The man was a dead ringer for the sketch Naomi had helped create of her leering man.

Leering man jumped behind the wheel of a dark gray pickup truck. Sawyer moved forward, trying to get a glimpse of the license plate. It was covered with mud.

Frustrated, Sawyer turned and ran back to the SUV.

No way was he letting this guy get away.

CHAPTER FIFTEEN

Naomi looked up in surprise when Sawyer came around the corner, running toward the SUV. She was about to get out of the vehicle when he yanked the door open and said, "I just saw leering guy."

She quickly closed her door in time for Sawyer to throw the gear shift into reverse to barrel out of their parking spot. "Where? At the motel?"

"At first, but now he's in a dark gray Chevy pickup truck with a muddy license plate." He pulled out his phone and tossed it into her lap. "Call 911, let them know."

She didn't hesitate to grab the phone Sawyer had handed her. As she explained to the dispatcher that they'd gotten a glimpse of the man in the sketch in a gray truck with muddy plates, she saw the vehicle up ahead. "There he is! We're on Highway 41 heading northwest."

"I'll have officers respond to the area," the dispatcher said in a calm voice. "Do not engage with the suspect."

Sawyer hit a pothole. She bounced in her seat and dropped the phone. Then he hit the brakes as the truck made a left turn, sending the phone beneath her seat.

She could hear the dispatcher talking but didn't want to take her eyes from the truck. It was far enough away that she could barely see the make and model, much less a license plate. Even if it hadn't been covered in mud. "Can you get close enough so I can see his face?"

Sawyer shook his head. "Right now, I just want to get him into custody. If it's not the right guy, fine. But if it is, I don't want him to slip away."

She could see his logic. The truck pulled off Highway 41 onto a smaller road. "Where is he going?"

"I'm not sure." Sawyer sped up a bit when the truck disappeared around a curve. "Maybe to where the girls are being kept?"

The thought of finding Kate filled her with hope, and she silently prayed God would guide them to her sister.

"I need the phone so we can let them know the truck has left the main highway." She bent over and reached beneath her seat, trying to find the device.

She couldn't hear the dispatcher's voice any longer and assumed their call had been disconnected. Where were the police? The dispatcher had claimed she'd send officers, but there was no sign of them.

Finally, she found the phone. Upon straightening in her seat, she frowned. "Where's the truck?"

"I don't know." Sawyer's voice was grim. "Look on your side for any sign of a driveway leading off this road."

Peering through the passenger-side window, she felt sick at the thick foliage. How would they ever find the truck? Leering man could have driven it anywhere.

Like a dead-end road, similar to the one where she'd managed to escape on that horrible night that seemed like eons ago rather than a few days.

And she had Sawyer and God to thank for saving her.

"I think I found it." Sawyer's voice broke into her thoughts.

"Where?" She craned her neck to look past him.

"I already passed it. Hang on." He slowed the SUV and made a Y turn in the road so they could head back. "Check out the driveway from your side. See it?"

"Yes." She swallowed hard. "But I don't see the truck."

"It's the only place where the truck could have pulled off, at least from what I can see." Sawyer pulled over to the side of the road and shut down the car. "I'm going to check it out."

"Wait." She grabbed his arm. "Don't go alone. Let's call for backup."

"I just want to see if the truck is there. If it is, then we'll get the police, okay?"

She didn't like it but slowly nodded. "Okay, but you have five minutes." She lifted the phone. "Then I'm calling them, even if the truck and leering man aren't here."

"Agreed. Keep the key fob, just in case." Sawyer dropped it into the cupholder, slid out from behind the wheel, and softly closed the door. She saw him reach down and grab something from his ankle, belatedly realizing it was a gun.

It made her feel better to know he was armed. But the thought that he might get into worse trouble quickly overwhelmed her.

Please, Lord, keep Sawyer safe in Your care!

She crawled over the console to get into the driver's seat. Sawyer was already gone from view, so she looked at the phone and made note of the time. He had five minutes, and not one second longer.

Was it possible this is where Kate and Louisa were being held? Other girls too?

She hoped and prayed if her sister was here, that she was all right.

The seconds ticked by slowly. One minute passed. Then another. She gripped the phone so tightly her knuckles went white. She wished the windows were down so she could hear better. But the only sound was her own ragged breathing and the rapid beat of her pulse.

Where was Sawyer? Had something happened to him? Had leering man found him and killed him?

As the last of the thirty seconds ticked by, a sick feeling of dread tightened in her gut. As she lifted the phone to her ear, the echo of a gunshot rang out.

No! Sawyer! She quickly pressed the call button, having already dialed in the 911. "Gunfire, on Canyon Road, off Highway 41. Repeat, shots fired!"

"I'm sending an officer to your location, please stay on the line."

Naomi didn't want to stay on the line. She wanted to run and find Sawyer. To see if Kate or Louisa were nearby.

But she also didn't want to make a bad situation worse. Melvin Curtis had used her as a hostage.

She wouldn't make that same mistake now.

She scrunched way down behind the wheel, breathing heavily as she strained to hear the sound of police sirens.

All she could do was pray.

SAWYER DUCKED as leering man fired his weapon in his direction. Sawyer had come all the way down the driveway to the cabin, but there was no sign of the pickup truck. At first he'd thought he had the wrong place, but then he'd gotten close enough to the dwelling to see movement inside.

And when he caught a glimpse of a young girl with dark hair, he'd felt certain he'd found Louisa.

Then gunfire had echoed around him. How in the world had leering man seen him? Unless the place was rigged with cameras? Something he should have considered before following the dirt road to the cabin.

Sawyer crouched in a dense thicket, planning his next move. He felt certain the gunfire would cause Naomi to call 911, which was good.

Unfortunately, he wasn't sure how long it would take for them to arrive. And he needed to get Louisa, if that's who he saw, out of the cabin.

Away from leering man.

There was nothing but silence for long seconds. No movement from inside the cabin either. Thanks to those weeks he, Cooper, and Trent had lived in the woods after escaping the fire, Sawyer was more comfortable in the woods than most. And, of course, living with the Preacher had taught all the foster kids the value of patience.

He felt certain he could outlast leering man. And found himself praying God would keep Louisa and Naomi safe.

There! A movement from the far side of the cabin. Leering man must be outside, waiting for him to make a move.

From this distance, his small gun wouldn't have the accuracy he desperately needed. With extreme caution, he eased toward the cabin, making sure not to draw leering man's attention.

One foot. Then another. He caught another glimpse of movement near the far corner of the cabin. Leering man was getting antsy.

A sense of grim satisfaction washed over him. Leering

man would be making his move, very soon. The guy wouldn't be able to help himself.

Sawyer planned to be ready. He didn't want to shoot the guy, his career was already on the line, but he wasn't going to risk Louisa's life either.

Or Naomi's.

It occurred to him that leering man might have called for someone to come help him. Or that there was someone inside the cabin, holding a weapon on Louisa.

That backup better get here soon.

Before it was too late.

Another flash of movement followed by the crack of gunfire. Sawyer saw a piece of bark fly off the tree where he'd been just a few minutes ago.

Good. Leering man thought he had Sawyer pinned down. Sawyer lifted a rock and tossed it at the same tree.

Another gunshot rang out. And Sawyer made another sliding move toward the cabin.

He was close to the building but still didn't see any movement inside. He needed to ease behind the structure, for cover and for the opportunity to get inside.

With another careful step, he managed to get behind the cabin, directly opposite from where leering man was hiding. Flattening himself against the wall, he edged to the window and peered through.

A bedroom, messy covers on the bed indicating it had been occupied recently.

He moved faster now, peering around the next corner. A back door faced more woods.

Without wasting another second, he ran in a crouch toward the door. Sirens wailed in the distance, far away but hopefully getting closer. He tried the door, surprised to find it wasn't locked.

He quickly opened the door and peered inside. No one waiting in the kitchen and living area. Then he heard the sound of someone moving through the brush and belatedly realized Louisa, or whoever was inside, may have already escaped out the back.

Silently shutting the door, he made his way to the next corner, knowing this was where leering man was hiding. He paused to listen.

The wail of sirens was louder now. Pressing his back to the wall, he lowered himself down, anticipating the guy would come around the corner to the back of the cabin at any moment.

But he was wrong. Instead, Sawyer heard the sound of a truck engine roaring to life.

No! Sawyer jumped up and ran around the corner in time to see the dark gray Chevy barreling out of a camouflaged shed toward the driveway. He fired at the rear window, shattering it, then attempted to hit the gas tank and at least one tire.

Red taillights flashed moments before he heard a loud gnashing of metal against metal. It took him a moment to realize Naomi had blocked the driveway with his SUV.

Sawyer ran forward. "Police! Come out with your hands up where I can see them!"

No movement from inside the truck. Knowing the guy was armed forced him to stay back.

"You're surrounded," he shouted. "Trust me, there is no chance to escape. We have the girl. Come out with your hands laced on the top of your head!"

The part about having Louisa was a lie, but he didn't care. He'd say whatever was necessary to convince leering man there was no hope to escape.

Another long pause as the sirens grew louder. Then

suddenly the driver's side door opened and leering man rolled out, firing his weapon as he hit the ground.

Sawyer ducked and returned fire. The guy let out a yell, but then fell silent.

Sawyer waited until several officers approached, wearing protective vests and helmets, before tossing his gun to the ground. He rose to his feet and placed his hands on his head. "I'm Sawyer Murphy, an off-duty cop!"

One of the armed cops came toward him. He recognized Tim Krill. "Sawyer? The lieutenant is going to have a fit when he hears about this."

Yeah, tell him something he didn't know. "Hey, Tim. How's the suspect?"

"He's alive, bleeding but alive," someone else called out. "Get the ambulance crew here ASAP."

He locked gazes with Officer Tim Krill. "You need to clear the cabin right away. I saw a young woman with dark hair inside, possibly our missing girl, Louisa Marchese. She may have escaped out the back as the rear door of the cabin wasn't locked." Sawyer continued standing with his hands on his head, unwilling to take any chances. "Please take a few men and fan out to search for her."

Krill glanced over to where a couple of officers shrugged and did as he'd asked.

"Sawyer?" Naomi emerged from the driver's seat of the SUV. "Are you okay?"

"I'll need to take your personal weapon," Krill said with a hint of apology in his tone. "At least for now."

"I know, it's okay, Tim." He lowered his hands and gestured for Naomi to stay put. "Nice move blocking him in, Naomi, but please get back inside the SUV until the area has been cleared."

She glanced at the cops who were already moving through the woods. "Okay, but I'm glad you weren't hurt."

"I'm glad you're safe too." He wanted nothing more than to run and hug her, but he forced himself to stay put. If Louisa was hiding in the woods, they needed to find her. To reassure her she was finally safe.

To let her know leering man would never hurt her again.

"I'd like to help search," Sawyer blurted. "Please, Tim, I promise I'm not going to run. You have my gun, and that's my SUV smashed up against the Chevy. I just want to find this girl."

"I don't know," Tim hedged.

"Cabin is clear!" an officer shouted from the front doorway. "Signs a female was here, but she's not now."

"You checked inside the truck?" Sawyer asked, even though he felt certain Louisa had escaped out the back of the cabin.

"It's empty," Krill confirmed. "The perp has sustained a belly wound, he's being taken to Parkridge East Hospital."

"You need to question him about Louisa Marchese and Kate Palmer," Sawyer urged. "Get him to spill his gut about what he knows about their disappearances."

Tim shrugged. "Not likely we'll be able to do that until he's been treated."

Sawyer hated knowing Tim was right. "Okay, then all the more reason we need to find Louisa, or whoever was being held inside the cabin."

Tim shuffled his feet, then sighed loudly. "Fine, you can help search."

"Thanks." Sawyer turned and hurried around to the back of the cabin. He felt certain Louisa had gone out the back door, likely taking a route that would take her as far from the gunfire as possible. A trajectory that would send her out at an angle from the cabin.

Sawyer had many life lessons that had been learned the hard way after escaping the Preacher. He'd become extremely proficient at tracking small game for food and to avoid becoming food for large game like mountain lions. He'd also learned to recognize human signs as a way to avoid being caught.

Tracking skills he'd put to good use now, searching intently for a sign of where Louisa had gone.

Or where she might be hiding.

He found a tuft of black fabric on a thorny bush. He honestly couldn't remember what color clothing Louisa had been wearing, he'd barely gotten a glimpse of her face. But he was encouraged that he was on the right track.

"Louisa? My name is Officer Murphy," he called, hoping the girl was within hearing distance. "Your mother, Francine, has been very worried about you."

No response.

He continued searching, reassured when he found a small footprint in the dirt at the base of a tree. Easy to imagine the young girl hiding there, catching her breath.

"Louisa, you're safe now." Sawyer swept his gaze over the area, trying to figure out which way she'd gone. "We have the man who kidnapped you in police custody. He's on his way to the hospital. I promise he can't hurt you anymore."

A rustle of leaves about twenty yards to his left caught his attention. He moved toward the area. "Were you alone? Or were there other girls with you? We want to find all of you. We'd like to bring everyone home to their respective families."

Another rustle of the leaves. He sensed the girl was

scared to death, wanting to believe him, but of course, he wasn't wearing his uniform either.

He wished Tim had come with him. "Officer Tim Krill?" Sawyer called out loudly, hoping his colleague was nearby. "Can you give me a hand?"

"Coming," was Tim's response.

Sawyer kept his hands visible so she could see he didn't have a weapon. "We have several police officers looking for you. I promise it's safe to come out of hiding."

Tim jogged over to where he stood, sounding like an elephant crashing through the brush. "Did you find her?"

"Yes. Louisa? This is Officer Tim Krill. We're not going to hurt you. Please come out."

Another rustle of leaves, then a pale face peeked through the branches. Soon, the frightened girl emerged from the bushes. She wore navy blue shorts and a black T-shirt, which was ripped in several places. Her arms and legs sported long scratches from her wild dash into the woods, and her long dark hair was tangled around her shoulders.

He easily recognized her from her mother's photograph. Louisa.

Thank you, God. His heart swelled with relief that they'd found her.

"Y-you talked to my mom?" Her gaze latched onto Sawyer's.

"I did, yes. She's been very worried about you." He wanted to hug her, but he kept his distance since he had no way of knowing what she'd been through.

The last thing she might want was to be touched by a man.

Tim stepped forward, but he put a hand on the officer's arm. "Easy. She's scared of men."

"Louisa?" Naomi's voice startled him. He turned to see

Naomi walking through the woods toward them. "My name is Naomi, and I've been searching for my sister, Kate."

"Katie?" Louisa came a few hesitant steps closer. "I know Katie. Katie and Paula."

Paula? The unknown female found dead in the woods?

"You know Katie?" Naomi's voice held a note of urgency. "Where is she?"

Louisa shook her head. "I don't know, the other guy came last night and took her away."

Other guy? Sawyer glanced at Naomi, then swung back to face Louisa. "What other guy? Can you tell us about him?"

Louisa's eyes filled with tears. "I—don't know his name, but he was really mean. Both of them were."

Naomi went pale but crossed over to lightly touch Louisa's arm. "It's okay, you're safe now. We're going to find the other guy, Kate, and Paula, you'll see."

Louisa threw herself into Naomi's arms, and the two girls stood in the woods, clinging to each other and sobbing.

As glad as he was to have found Louisa, he wouldn't rest until they'd brought Kate home too.

CHAPTER SIXTEEN

Tears streamed down her face as she held Louisa. The girl appeared younger than Kate and had obviously been through a lot. Unimaginable horrors.

She drew in several breaths to calm herself. This wasn't the time to fall apart, no matter how much she wanted to. Louisa needed to be treated for her emotional and physical trauma, and hopefully the girl could give a description of the other man.

The one who still had her sister, Kate.

"Louisa? There are EMTs here to take you to the hospital." Sawyer's voice came from behind her. She gently pulled away from the girl but kept one hand on the girl's slim shoulders, feeling certain the girl needed a female touch.

"I don't wanna go to the hospital," Louisa whispered.

"Louisa, honey, I know how hard this is for you." Naomi chose her words, carefully. "I'm sorry you had to go through this. But it's really important for you to be examined so the police can press charges against the man who hurt you."

Naomi caught and held the girl's gaze. "You don't want him to get away with what he's done, do you?"

"N-no." Louisa gripped her arm. "Will you come with me? Please?"

She glanced back at Sawyer who nodded his approval. "Yes, I'll come with you. Ready to go?"

Louisa sniffled, swiped at her face, and nodded. Naomi put an arm around the girl and walked alongside her to where Sawyer and a second officer waited.

"Louisa, this is Officer Krill," Sawyer said gently. "At some point he'll need to talk to you, okay?"

"Okay, but I want Naomi to stay with me."

The officer looked uncomfortable with that scenario, but Sawyer quickly spoke up. "Sure, that's fine. We're going to call your mom too."

Fresh tears brimmed in the girl's eyes. "Yes, I want my mom."

"I'm sure your mother will meet us at the hospital," Naomi assured her, glancing once again at Sawyer.

"Do you think the unknown female—"

Sawyer cut off what the officer was about to say. "Not now, Tim. We'll have time to check into that later."

"Unknown female?" Louisa had gone pale.

"Nothing for you to worry about," Naomi assured her. "You're safe now. And the man who did this will be going to jail for a very long time."

The girl shivered but didn't say anything else. The EMTs joined them. The female tech unfolded a blanket and curled it around Louisa.

Naomi was glad there would be a woman taking care of Louisa. The way the girl hovered close, it was easy to see how traumatized she was.

Naomi knew in that moment this was what she was

facing with Kate. As horrible as it sounded, it was highly likely that her sister had been treated the same way as Louisa.

Leaving Sawyer back at the crime scene wasn't easy, but it was more important to stay with Louisa. The male EMT climbed in behind the wheel, leaving the female EMT named Stephanie and Naomi in the back.

Naomi held Louisa's hand as Stephanie took a set of vital signs, asking the girl basic questions about her health. The trip to Parkridge East Hospital didn't seem to take long, or maybe it was just that Stephanie helped make the time go by faster.

Once they were settled in an exam room, Louisa's grip tightened around her hand. "I don't want them to check me out," she whispered.

Naomi's heart broke for the girl. She could only imagine how difficult this would be. "Do you want to wait for your mother to arrive?"

The girl hesitated, then shook her head. "I don't want my mom to know . . ."

"Louisa, your mom loves you very much. None of this is your fault. You didn't do anything wrong, okay? This isn't going to change your mother's feelings toward you."

"I—sneaked out of my house," Louisa whispered. "I left a note and was going to meet up with my boyfriend, but then a white van pulled up next to me. A man grabbed me. I didn't want to go with him, but he was so strong . . ."

"Louisa, listen to me. Sneaking out of your house doesn't mean you asked for this to happen. The men who took you are evil and need to be thrown in jail."

A sweet middle-aged nurse came in and introduced herself as Mary. Louisa tearfully endured the initial physical exam, and then the rape kit. When it was over, she curled into a ball, still holding on to Naomi's hand.

Less than five minutes later, a woman who looked like an older version of Louisa came into the room. "My baby," she cried.

"Mama!" Louisa finally let go of Naomi's hand to embrace her mother. Naomi slipped out the door, leaving the two of them alone in the room.

She leaned against the wall for a moment, staring down at her feet. Hopefully, Louisa would recover from this with the help of her mother's love and counseling.

Kate would too.

But first they had to find her.

She pushed away from the wall when Officer Tim Krill and Sawyer approached. She met Sawyer's compassionate gaze and gave a tiny nod.

"Rape kit has been completed." An ordeal that would haunt Naomi almost as much as Louisa. "Her mother is in with her now."

"Did she give you any more information on the other guy who took Kate?" Sawyer asked.

"No. But I didn't push either. She was going through enough without me adding to it."

Sawyer took her hand and gently squeezed it. "Thanks for your help with Louisa."

Having done what any woman would have, she simply nodded. "I'm so worried about Kate."

"I know." Sawyer continued holding her hand. "I'm sure Louisa will be able to help with a description of the guy."

"Yeah, maybe." The thought wasn't encouraging. She'd given the sketch of leering man, and that hadn't helped as much as she'd hoped.

Except that Sawyer had recognized him. And based on that, they were able to find the cabin, and ultimately Louisa.

Officer Tim Krill poked his head out of the hospital room. "Ms. Palmer? Louisa would like you to be here when I question her."

"Please call me Naomi." She released Sawyer's hand and joined Officer Krill in the room.

The questioning didn't take long, mostly because Louisa couldn't remember much. She'd been held in the cabin for most of her time with leering man. He kept her tied to the bed after Paula had escaped. Today, she'd managed to escape the binds. She'd been too afraid to run, until she heard gunfire.

Naomi tried not to show her dismay at the news. Paula hadn't escaped, not really. She'd ended up murdered, if she was the same girl that had been found in the woods.

"What can you tell us about the other man?" Officer Krill asked. "Is he tall or short? Fat or thin? What color is his hair?"

Louisa cuddled closer to her mother. "He was tall, skinny, and had light hair." She shivered, then added, "What I remember the most was his mean eyes."

"What color were his eyes?" Krill pressed.

Louisa shook her head. "I don't know, he mostly came at night."

No one spoke for a long moment. Finally, Naomi stepped forward and crouched down next to Louisa's bed. "Louisa, when was the last time you saw the other man and Katie? How many days ago?"

"Last night."

"Did the other man say where he was taking Kate?" she asked.

"No, just that he wanted to take Katie someplace else."

Louisa's dark gaze clung to hers. "You're going to find Katie and Paula, right?"

"Yes, we will. Thanks for giving us this information, it will help a lot." Naomi forced a smile and glanced up at Francine. "Your daughter is strong, but she'll need counseling. I plan to have Kate go through counseling, too, once we get her home."

"I know. Thanks for helping find her." Francine looked as if she wanted to cry.

Naomi stood and walked from the room. Louisa had seen Kate less than twenty-four hours ago. The news was both encouraging and frustrating. If they'd have found the cabin a day earlier . . .

No, there was no point in going down the what-if road.

She tried to take heart in the fact that her sister was alive and in East Ridge less than twenty-four hours ago.

There was still time to find her.

If they only knew where to look.

SAWYER LISTENED as Krill asked Louisa a few more questions, but it was clear the girl had told them everything she knew.

He stepped forward, glancing at Francine, then down at Louisa. "You might think of something later, so please don't hesitate to call Officer Krill, okay? Any small detail could help us find Katie."

"Okay," Louisa agreed.

He left the room, hoping to find Naomi. He was relieved to see she was waiting in the hallway.

Before he could say anything, another man came toward

them. He straightened when he recognized Detective Turner.

"Murphy," Dewayne Turner greeted him with a solemn nod. "Good work finding Louisa."

No thanks to you, he thought wearily. Still, this was the most professional Turner had been toward him, so he forced himself to be polite. "Thanks. Any word on the injured perp?"

Turner nodded. "He's in surgery, but it sounds like he'll recover. Hopefully soon enough to tell us what he knows about the other guy and Kate Palmer."

"Louisa mentioned a girl by the name of Paula who had managed to escape," Naomi said. "She might be the girl who was found dead nearby."

"I heard. The reason it took me so long to get here is that I checked the missing person's data bank. A girl named Paula Rivers was reported missing from Chatsworth, Georgia, five days ago." Turner glanced at Naomi, then back at Sawyer. "We're in the process of requesting her dental records to match up with our Jane Doe."

It seemed as if Turner was finally putting the pieces of the puzzle together. Why it took him this long, Sawyer had no clue. "Great. Don't let Louisa know we believe Paula is dead. She has enough to deal with right now."

"I won't," the detective agreed.

"Do you have an ID on the guy in surgery?" Sawyer figured it couldn't hurt to ask.

"Yeah, we ran his prints before he was whisked off to surgery," Turner replied. "His name is William Evers, goes by Billy. He has a rap sheet significant for soliciting prostitution."

Sawyer turned to Naomi. "Does that name mean anything to you?"

"No." She looked depressed at the news. "I wish it did."

"Did his prints match those on the shanty?" Sawyer asked.

"No." Turner moved past them to the doorway, then turned back. "Murphy, what about that motel where you saw the guy in the sketch? Do you think the motel is involved in some way?"

Sawyer thought back. "Yeah, maybe. Although I don't think Louisa was in the truck when I followed it."

"It just seems odd," Turner muttered. "Either he was looking for another girl to snatch or he was looking for some guy who might want to have sex with an underage girl."

Naomi shivered, and he moved closer so that he could take her hand. "Good point. Maybe you should take a team of cops there to check things out."

"I will as soon as I'm finished, here. The lieutenant is getting a team together now, and the FBI will be arriving shortly to take over." Turner seemed glad to hand the case over, and Sawyer realized the detective must have been overwhelmed by the complicated case. It was likely why he kept trying to simplify things by going after the boyfriend angle. Maybe he'd spent so much time on details because that was easy for him to do. Sawyer watched as the detective entered Louisa's room.

"I want to go back to that motel," Naomi said in a low voice. "The third guy involved in this might have her there."

"Hold on, Naomi. I don't have a weapon, and I'm still on paid leave. I'm already on thin ice from the incident at the cabin. We need to leave this in the hands of the police and the Feds."

"But what if Kate is there now? She could be gone by the time the cops arrive."

He hated disappointing her. Worse, he silently agreed

with heading to the motel. It had been bugging him that he'd found leering man, AKA Billy Evers, there.

"Please, Sawyer." Naomi put her hand on his arm. "We need to find Kate."

She was impossible to resist. He raked his hand through his short hair and nodded. "Okay, fine. But first I need to go back to my place. I can't go near that motel unarmed."

Her eyes widened. "You have three guns?"

"Shh." He winced. "The weapon I'm going to pick up isn't exactly legal." He didn't want to mention how he'd bought it from some gun dealer years ago, the serial numbers having been filed off. It was after he'd been nearly killed by a group of thugs on the street and before Joe Kohl had taken him in.

Living with Joe who was a cop, Sawyer knew he should have gotten rid of the illegal weapon a long time ago. At the time, he'd hung on to it, wanting backup in case he ever had to go on the run again. In the back of his mind, he'd always worried he'd have to take off from Joe's place to start over someplace new. In the years he'd been on the police force, he'd still kept the gun. Maybe because the kid in him still wanted some way to protect himself from some unknown threat. Stupid and crazy since being found with an illegal gun could end his career.

Sawyer felt certain he'd prevail in the shooting of Melvin Curtis and William Evers. But being in possession of an illegal weapon would be impossible to explain away.

He glanced at the door to Louisa's room. By the time he went back to his place, then returned to the motel, he figured Turner would have the police and the Feds there as well.

And if they found Kate, the young girl would be more

comfortable with Naomi than with a slew of strange men, even if they were cops.

"Come on, let's go." He took Naomi's arm and headed out of the emergency department. He led her to his badly dented SUV.

"How did you get your car back?"

"They took photos of the two vehicles together and let it go at that." He figured Officer Krill and the others were cutting him a break since he'd helped find Louisa. "Thankfully, the engine runs, its entire passenger side took the brunt of the collision. You'll have to go in through the driver's side."

"I was worried the airbags would deploy, but apparently I wasn't going fast enough for that." Naomi crawled over the console, then dropped into the passenger seat.

He followed her into the vehicle and headed back toward Chattanooga.

"Sawyer, are you sure about this?" Naomi's voice held a tinge of doubt. "I don't want you to get into trouble."

Her concern was touching. "I'm sure." He wasn't and privately hoped the Feds would beat them to the motel.

Naomi looked concerned but didn't say anything more as he made the drive back to his cabin. Returning to his place was a risk, but now that William Evers, AKA leering man, was in the hospital, he wasn't too worried. After all, the other guy had taken off with Kate.

Hopefully not out of state. He didn't like knowing Paula had been from Chatsworth, Kate from Dalton, and Louisa here in East Ridge.

A sex-trafficking ring that crossed two state lines, and maybe more. He doubted Paula, Louisa, and Kate had been the first girls taken by this crew.

But he silently promised they would be the last.

He increased his speed, wanting to get to the motel shortly after the Feds and local cops did. Hopefully, he wouldn't need his unregistered weapon.

But he couldn't go near danger empty-handed.

He slowed the SUV to enter his long driveway. The vehicle bounced up and down over the rocky terrain more than usual, and he suspected there was structural damage to the SUV as well.

Not that it mattered. Capturing Evers and finding Louisa had been well worth it.

"Stay here and wait for me." He glanced at Naomi as he shut down the engine. "This won't take long."

She rested her hand on his arm. "Last chance to back out, Sawyer. You don't have to do this. I really don't want you to get in trouble."

"I'll be fine, don't worry." He smiled and slid out of the driver's seat. Before going inside, he made a quick detour to check on his trip wires.

They didn't appear disturbed. Reassured, he turned toward his cabin.

As he inserted the key into the lock, the front door abruptly opened, revealing a tall thin man with blond hair, holding a gun leveled at his chest.

Sawyer froze, especially when he caught a glimpse of a young girl sitting inside tied to one of his kitchen chairs.

"Get Naomi."

At first, the stranger's request didn't make any sense. How did this guy know Naomi's name?

"I want Naomi, now. Get her or I'll shoot you where you stand." The skinny guy didn't look as if he were on drugs or suffering from mental illness. His eyes were cold and steady.

Sawyer tensed. This was not going to end well. Especially since he didn't have a gun.

"Tony? What are you doing?"

Naomi's shout came from directly behind him, which means she'd gotten out of the car. Still, Sawyer didn't dare take his gaze from the gunman. Then it clicked. Naomi knew this guy. He was her former boyfriend.

"Get over here, Naomi, or the cop dies. And your sister too."

No! Don't do it! Stay back! Sawyer willed Naomi to jump into the car and drive away. He didn't dare move, keeping a wary eye on Tony's trigger finger.

Sawyer was unarmed and too close to the guy to avoid being shot. All he could do was sacrifice himself to save Naomi and Kate. He sent up a silent prayer for God to watch over the two women. A strange sense of calm washed over him.

"It was you?" Naomi shouted incredulously. "All this time, it was you? Why did you have to drag Kate into this, Tony, huh? Why not just take me?"

"I wanted you, but you left me." Tony's trigger finger tightened but then relaxed, the perp's gaze seemingly focused on Naomi. "Now, Naomi!"

Movement from behind Sawyer made him tense, and then he heard a series of strange thuds, like something hitting the ground, then another something hitting a tree. Sawyer watched as the tip of the gun wavered, then moved away from him.

Now.

Taking advantage of the distraction, Sawyer dropped, rolled, and kicked Tony below the belt. A gunshot rang out at the exact moment the guy howled. Sawyer kicked again, managing to hit Tony's gun hand. The weapon flew into the brush. Tony was doubled over in pain but kicked out at Sawyer. Ignoring the impact to his kidney, Sawyer leapt to his feet and brought both of his fists down on the back of Tony's head.

The man teetered for a moment, then fell to the ground. Sawyer grabbed both of Tony's wrists and yanked them together. He didn't have a pair of handcuffs in his pocket, but it didn't matter.

Tony groaned and went limp.

Sawyer dropped his chin to his chest. Three for three.

It was over.

CHAPTER SEVENTEEN

Heart lodged in her throat, Naomi ran toward Sawyer and the supine form of Tony Baldwin. She hadn't known what to do to draw Tony's attention away from Sawyer, so she'd stupidly performed a backflip, followed by a cartwheel, and then she picked a rock up off the ground and threw it into the woods.

The moves hadn't been pretty, her aim off, but the rather pathetic attempt was all she could think of to distract Tony. She'd been so shocked to discover Tony was involved she'd gotten out of the car and approached him without even realizing what she'd done.

Sawyer had almost been shot because of her. The horror of almost losing him forever made her head spin.

"Naomi, are you all right?"

His concern was humbling. "I'm fine, but what about you?" She frantically scanned him for signs of injury.

"I'm okay. Go inside, check on your sister."

Kate was inside? Naomi rushed through the open doorway. Her stomach lurched when she saw her half sister, Kate, seated in one of Sawyer's kitchen chairs, tied and gagged. Kate's eyes were wide and frantic as she struggled against the bindings.

"Shh, it's okay, you're safe now." She removed the gag first, then fought the knots. But they were extremely tight. She ran around the kitchen table, grabbed a knife from the butcher block on the counter, and quickly cut the rope digging into her sister's skin.

"H-how did you find me?" Kate's voice was hoarse, as if she'd been gagged for a while.

"It's a long story. How long have you been here?" Naomi couldn't imagine what would have happened if they hadn't shown up when they did.

"I-I'm not sure. It seemed like hours." Kate moaned when Naomi cut her arms free. "Hurts."

"I know, I'm sorry." Tears pricked her eyes, but she concentrated on cutting the binds around her sister's feet. Then she took the remains of the rope out to Sawyer. "Can you use these to tie him up?"

"Yes, thanks." Sawyer was still holding Tony's wrists.

"Is he—unconscious?" Naomi stared down at Tony's limp body.

Sawyer glanced up at her as he bound Tony's wrists tightly together. "Yes, but he'll survive. How's your sister?"

"She'll survive too." Naomi returned to the kitchen, crouching beside her sister. "Listen, Kate, we'll need to take you to the hospital, okay?"

"No need, I'm fine." Kate's words were brave, but her lower lip trembled, and bright tears filled her eyes.

"It's okay." Naomi gathered her sister close, offering as much reassurance as possible. "You're going to get through this, Kate. I'll do whatever I can to help you get through this."

Kate leaned against her, burying her face in her chest.

"It's my fault," she whispered. "I went with Tony. I wanted to be with him."

Naomi hugged her sister tight. "You're only sixteen, Kate. It's not your fault. Tony is a monster who preyed on young girls." It made her sick to realize she'd actually dated the guy.

Bile rose in the back of Naomi's throat. She fought the urge to throw up, focusing on Kate. Her sister needed her to be strong.

"I thought he liked me." Kate's words were muffled. "I thought it was cool that he liked me more than you. Only then I realized he only wanted me for sex and expected me to be with other men too." Her slim shoulders shook with sobs.

"Oh, Kate." Naomi closed her eyes against a fresh wave of tears and rested her cheek on her sister's head. "I'm sorry. So sorry. I wish there was something I could do to change what happened to you."

"He was obsessed with you, Naomi."

She suppressed a shiver. "He didn't get to me."

"Kate?" Sawyer's deep voice caused Kate to sit up. He gently draped a blanket around her shoulders, which Kate gratefully gathered close. "We found Louisa; she's safe too."

"Louisa?" Hope flared in Kate's amber eyes as she looked from Sawyer to Naomi. "She's okay?"

"Yes." Sawyer pulled up a chair, careful to keep some distance between him and her sister. "We arrested Billy Evers. He was working with Tony, right?"

Kate sniffled and nodded.

"Louisa was scared, just like you. But she went to the hospital to be checked out, to help us send Billy to jail for a long time."

Naomi felt Kate flinch, but that didn't stop her from

tagging onto Sawyer's request. "Kate, Tony needs to be put in jail too. He should pay for what he did to you, and to all girls, right? You don't want him to go free, do you?"

"No." Kate's voice was barely a whisper. She clutched the blanket as if it was a lifeline. "He deserves to be locked up the way he kept us locked up."

Hearing firsthand what her sister had been through was the most difficult thing Naomi endured. Even losing her mother hadn't been this hard. It was all she could do not to go over and pummel Tony with her fists.

"Will you allow us to take you to the hospital?" Sawyer asked gently. "The police are on their way to pick up Tony. Once they take him to jail, we can head over there."

Kate hesitated for a long moment, before whispering, "Yes. I'll go to the hospital."

Naomi closed her eyes and silently thanked God for helping them find Kate. Her sister had a long road ahead, but this would be the first step of the healing process.

At least, Naomi hoped so. She'd need to find a counselor in the Dalton area for Kate as soon as possible.

The sound of a car approaching had Sawyer rising to his feet. He briefly rested his hand on Naomi's shoulder, squeezing it reassuringly, before heading outside.

Naomi placed her arm around Kate's shoulders, hugging her. "We'll be home soon. I promise."

Kate nodded but didn't say anything more. Naomi glanced over to where Sawyer was talking to a uniformed officer, no doubt describing what had happened here.

The nightmare was finally over. Sawyer had risked his career, and his very life, to help her.

Without Sawyer, she never would have found Kate. She owed him so much . . .

She loved him.

The realization was stunning, yet she couldn't do anything about it. For a brief moment, she lifted her gaze to the ceiling, imagining God up there watching over them.

She loved Sawyer and hated the thought of leaving him, but she couldn't stay. Her sister's health and well-being had to be her top priority.

Maybe one day . . .

"Let go of me." Tony's low, gravelly voice carried into the cabin. "That jerk knocked me unconscious. I want him arrested for assault."

Kate abruptly threw off the blanket and sprang to her feet. She stumbled toward the doorway.

"You hurt me!" she screamed before slamming her hands against his chest. "I hate you!"

Naomi rushed forward and pulled Kate away from the handcuffed man. "Don't, Kate, he's not worth it. Your testimony will put him in jail for the rest of his life."

"He told me he wanted to use me to get to you, Naomi." Kate stared at Tony with revulsion. "He couldn't believe you broke up with him." Kate sniffled. "He also tried to have sex with Paula, and when she escaped, he chased her through the woods. Only he came back alone, telling us that if we didn't listen to him, we'd end up like Paula."

Naomi's gaze clashed with Sawyers. "Us? You and Louisa?" Naomi asked.

Kate nodded.

"You saw him chase Paula through the woods?" Sawyer asked.

"Yes." Kate stared defiantly at Tony. "She wasn't wearing any clothes when she ran outside."

Tony's mouth formed a grim line, and Naomi couldn't help but feel a surge of satisfaction. Tony knew his life was over, and she was proud of her sister for stepping forward with the additional information they needed to put the final nail in his coffin.

"Arrest him for murder, kidnapping, and sexual assault of a minor," Sawyer said to the officer who'd grabbed Tony's arm.

"My pleasure," the officer said, yanking Tony to the squad. "Tony Baldwin, you have the right to remain silent. Anything you say can and will be used against you in a court of law."

Naomi tuned out the rest of the Miranda warning as she looked at Sawyer. "Can we please take Kate to the hospital now?"

"Of course." He went back inside for the blanket, closed and locked the door, then returned to the SUV. Naomi climbed into the back seat so she could be next to Kate.

The road ahead would be difficult and long, but each step would take them one step closer to healing.

She prayed for God to continue to watch over Kate as her sister endured what was yet to come.

***

SAWYER BATTLED a wave of exhaustion as he sat in the emergency department waiting room for Naomi and Kate. The doctor had already finished, but Officer Krill was taking Kate's statement.

There were still many details of the investigation that needed to be answered. The pink hair band didn't belong to Kate, but the partial print at the shanty was a match to Tony Baldwin. Sawyer believed the shanty had been a temporary holding cell, used to hand the girls off from one person to the next. It would explain why Curtis and Evers had planned to take Naomi there.

A team of officers had gone to the motel and arrested the manager who'd admitted to renting his rooms to be used for so-called *entertainment* services. He claimed he didn't know anything about underage girls or anyone paying for sex, but Sawyer figured the guy would change his tune, ready to tell every last gory detail, once he'd been locked up for a while.

He still couldn't believe they'd found Louisa and Kate. In those moments outside his cabin, he'd actually felt God's presence. Something he'd never experienced before in his life.

The Preacher had lied during his screaming sermons about how God would punish them. Sawyer wasn't sure why he and the others had to suffer at the Preacher's hands any more than he understood why Kate and Louisa had suffered at the hands of Baldwin, Curtis, and Evers.

Maybe Naomi was right about how God's plan wasn't theirs to understand but to accept His guidance while continuing to honor Him.

He couldn't deny God had watched over them. Today and hopefully forever more.

After what seemed like an eternity, Krill entered the waiting room and crossed over to him. The guy looked sick, as if interviewing two traumatized teenagers in one day had taken a toll. Sawyer couldn't blame the guy.

Krill gave him a nod. "Nice work taking down Tony Baldwin."

"He held me at gunpoint, but somehow Naomi distracted him enough so I could disarm him."

A lopsided smile tugged at the cop's mouth. "Flips and cartwheels, then throwing a rock."

Sawyer blinked. "Excuse me?"

Krill shrugged. "Hey, that's what she told me. Naomi is

apparently a former gymnast and cheerleader. She couldn't think of what to do, so she did a backflip, followed by a cartwheel moving to the side, and then tossing a rock to distract Baldwin."

Sawyer remembered the weird sounds and the moment the tip of the gun moved away from him. "Well, crazy as it sounds, it worked."

"Any idea why the guy was at your cabin in the first place?"

Sawyer grimaced. "I never expected him to be there, especially not with Kate. I did know, though, that someone found my cabin, as I had an intruder outside take shots at me. And there were shots fired earlier this morning when we were leaving the cabin. They must have known Naomi was staying there with me, at least when we weren't staying in town."

Krill eyed him curiously. "I thought for sure you would show up at the motel."

Ironic that he had returned to his cabin to get an illegal weapon only to stumble across Baldwin. "I wanted to meet you there, but I wasn't armed and didn't want to put Naomi in danger." He left out the part about his intent to pick up his illegal gun.

Krill nodded. "I can see that."

Sawyer made a silent promise to get rid of the unlicensed gun the minute he returned home. No more looking backward. It was time to move forward. He gestured toward the hospital exam rooms. "How are they holding up?"

"Surprisingly well," Krill acknowledged. He scrubbed his hands over his face.

"There might be other girls out there," Sawyer said. "We'll need to lean on that motel manager to get more information."

"The lieutenant and the Feds are all over it." Krill stood. "Detective Turner is being demoted for being too slow, too mired in details to do the job well enough to satisfy the lieutenant. Apparently the boss is looking for someone who has already taken the detective exam to replace him."

Sawyer glanced up in surprise. He'd taken the exam, but Turner had gotten the job. "Oh yeah?"

"The lieutenant wanted you to know." Krill smiled as he turned away.

Becoming a detective had long been a goal of his, but that was something to think about for another day.

Right now, he had two women to look after. He crossed over to the desk and asked to see Kate Palmer. When he entered the room, he saw that Naomi and Kate were still huddled close together.

"Hey, are you ready to get out of here?"

"Yes, but I have a favor to ask." Naomi glanced at him nervously. "I need you to see if my car has been repaired so I can take Kate home."

Home to Dalton, Sawyer knew. His chest tightened, but he'd expected this. "I'll drive you home and will arrange for your car to be transported when it's ready."

"You will?" Naomi looked surprised.

"Of course." He wanted to pull her into his arms, but Kate needed Naomi more than he needed to kiss her.

Maybe.

"Thanks, Sawyer." Naomi gently eased from Kate. "Why don't you get dressed in the bathroom?"

"Okay." Kate took the clothes Naomi had folded. "I'd like to take a shower if that's okay."

"Yes, of course. Take your time," Naomi urged.

Kate nodded and disappeared into the bathroom.

"You are incredible," Sawyer murmured. He lifted a

hand to tuck a strand of hair behind her ear. "I wouldn't have been able to disarm Baldwin without your help."

She flushed. "I should have stayed in the car."

"No, don't even think like that." He took a step closer, holding her gaze. "God was watching over us, Naomi. And we found Kate, which is all that matters."

"Yes, I know." Naomi's smile was tenuous. "It could have ended so much worse, still, Kate has been through so much . . ."

"Shh." He couldn't bear being separated from her a second longer. He gathered Naomi close, cradling her against him. "She's strong, like you. It won't be easy, but she'll recover. Just like Louisa."

A chance Paula hadn't been given.

"Sawyer, I don't know what I'd have done without you." Naomi pressed her face into the hollow of his neck.

"I love you," he whispered.

She went still. "What?"

He managed to smile. "I love you, Naomi. I understand you and Kate are a package deal, and that you'll need some time to heal from all of this, but I'm willing to wait. For as long as it takes."

"Sawyer." Naomi lifted her head and gazed up at him. "I love you, too, but it feels wrong to be happy at a time when Kate is suffering so much. And I can't help but think it's my fault. If I hadn't dated Tony in the first place . . ."

"Hey, you had nothing to do with this." He was secretly thrilled she'd admitted she loved him, yet he understood more than anyone what it was like to experience survivor's guilt. Naomi had escaped Curtis and Evers when Kate hadn't. "Remember how I told you about the pokeweed berries I hid in the pie? How he and Ruth had eaten the blueberry pie and subsequently died in the fire?"

Her brow furrowed. "That's hardly the same thing."

"You told me that I had nothing to feel guilty about, right? And you insisted God forgives all sins," he continued. "Don't you think the same applies to you?"

She stared at him for a long moment. "Maybe."

"Did you have any idea Tony was involved in sex trafficking?"

"No!" Her denial was swift. "I'd have turned him in to the authorities in a heartbeat. I thought he was a jerk, pressuring me to sleep with him, but I never imagined he could do something like this. Especially not become obsessed with me because I refused him."

"Exactly. You didn't have anything to do with his actions. In fact, God was probably trying to tell you to stay away from him. And you listened to those instincts that warned you he was bad news."

"Yeah, so he could turn his attention to Kate."

"If not Kate, likely some other girl." Her tortured gaze ripped at his soul. "We're still figuring out all the details surrounding these events, but I believe Baldwin, Curtis, and Evers had quite the scheme going. Pick up a few girls, get them to have sex with strangers for money at the motel, then move them along to another group of men. Tony's big mistake was lashing out at you by seducing and then kidnapping Kate. If you hadn't followed the white van, they may have gotten away with it." He hesitated, then added, "Think of all the girls you've saved, Naomi. And once this investigation is finished, there could be even more girls reunited with their families."

Her expression softened. "You're right. I need to try and stay positive."

"Yes, you do. Kate will need you to be strong, Naomi. And I want to be there with you both to help as needed."

"Oh, Sawyer. That's a generous offer, but this is going to take time. You have a good career here. I can't ask you to give it up. Especially since Dalton, carpet capital of the world, doesn't have much to offer."

"My career isn't as important as you and Kate." He gathered her close. "We'll work out the details later. I love you, and I'm not going to let you go. If you want to stay in Dalton, that's fine. Or we can live here, in Chattanooga. It doesn't matter to me one way or the other. For now, we'll focus on one step at a time. And don't forget, I'm on leave of absence for the next few days." He offered a crooked grin. "It would be an honor to drive you and Kate home."

"I love you so much," Naomi whispered, before reaching up to wrap her arms around his neck. "I'm not sure what I did to deserve it, but you're the best thing that's ever happened to me."

"Same goes," he whispered, before capturing her mouth in a deep kiss.

"Oh, so you two are—together?" Kate's question ended their kiss.

"You don't have to worry about me and Sawyer," Naomi hastened to reassure her. "All you need to do is to focus on healing."

Sawyer looked at the sixteen-year-old who suddenly looked much older than her years. He held Kate's gaze. "I love your sister, very much. But I won't take her away from you, Kate. There's no rush. We have plenty of time."

Kate nodded, then glanced at Naomi. "I don't want to go back to work at the carpet factory."

"You don't have to," Naomi assured her.

"There isn't much else to offer in Dalton." Kate swung to face Sawyer. "My sister hates her job at the clinic, so maybe you could work something out so that she can find a critical care job here in Chattanooga. I like it better here than in Dalton."

"You do?" Naomi sounded shocked. "Even after everything you've been through?"

Kate grimaced and stared down at the floor. "Yes," she said softly. "You have to understand I went along with Tony at first; it was only later that I realized what was going on." She lifted her gaze to Naomi. "I think we should sell the house and relocate here. Start with a clean slate."

"Something to think about," Sawyer said diplomatically. "But for now, let's just go home."

"Home is wherever the heart is," Naomi whispered.

He put his arm around her shoulders. Yes, home was where the heart is.

And his heart was with Naomi.

EPILOGUE

Two weeks later...

Sawyer had moved Kate and Naomi temporarily into his cabin so he could return to work. The women shared the guest room. Kate still suffered from nightmares, and Naomi wanted to be at her side.

He'd been cleared of any wrongdoing in the deadly shooting of Curtis and the shooting and subsequent abdominal injury to Evers. The latter survived and began to talk once he knew Baldwin had been arrested. Curtis apparently had a connection in Nashville. They brought girls who were runaways or girls who were easily swayed by Tony Baldwin's good looks to Chattanooga where they began the sex-trafficking ring. From there, they often sent the girls to Nashville, heading back down to Atlanta and other cities along the way to get new girls.

Now that the Chattanooga connection had been shut down, his boss and the FBI were searching for the source in Nashville. His boss had also promoted Sawyer to detective the minute he'd been cleared in his role in the shootings. Frankly, Turner had seemed relieved to be back on patrol.

And Sawyer knew the lieutenant would keep a close eye on him to make sure he was doing a good job.

Sawyer had the weekend off and was trying to think of something to do with Naomi and Kate as they needed a distraction from recent events. His phone rang, and his heart jumped a bit when he recognized Hailey's number.

"Hailey? Is that you?"

"Sawyer, I'm so glad to hear your voice. Are you at work?"

"Nope, I have the weekend off. Why?"

"I'm in downtown Chattanooga with a friend of mine, Rock Wilson." He heard mumbling in the background. "Okay, well actually, Rock is more than a friend. He's my fiancé."

"Congrats, Hailey, you deserve to be happy." His smile widened. "I can't believe you drove all the way from Gatlinburg without knowing if I was working or not. I thought we were going to coordinate our schedules?"

"I couldn't wait," Hailey confessed. "I have the whole week off, so I figured you must have at least one or two days off in a week." She laughed, a sound he'd never heard before. "This is my first vacation in—well, forever."

He sensed movement behind him and smiled at Naomi who stood near the stove. She was smiling, and he figured she'd overheard most if not all of the conversation.

"Hailey, I'd love to see you and Rock too. I, uh, have guests staying with me, so I hope you don't mind if I bring them along."

"Some of our foster siblings?" Hailey's voice rose with excitement.

"No, unfortunately." He really needed to work harder to find the other foster kids who'd escaped the Preacher thirteen years ago. "Naomi, who happens to be a very special woman in my life, and her younger sister, Kate."

"The more the merrier," Hailey said. "You sound happy, Sawyer."

"I am." His gaze clung to Naomi's. "Give me an hour or so and we'll meet up with you, okay?"

"Sounds great, I can't wait to see you." Hailey disconnected from the call.

"Hailey is one of your foster sisters, right?" Naomi asked.

"Yeah, we've been in touch a few times lately." He stood and went over to pull her into his arms. "I'll understand if you and Kate would rather stay here. I can always catch up with Hailey and Rock later."

"No, I think it will be good for Kate to get out for a bit. She's been spending way too much time in your vegetable garden." Naomi wound her arms around his neck and kissed him. "And I can't wait to meet your sister."

His heart swelled with love. "Naomi, would you please marry me? Not now, but when Kate is feeling better?" He held her gaze. "I love you, and I don't want to live my life without you."

"Yes, Sawyer. I'd be honored to marry you. Once Kate is doing better," she added.

"Hey, don't let me stand in the way," Kate said from the hallway.

Sawyer released Naomi and faced his soon-to-be sister-in-law. "Kate, I told you before, there's no rush."

"You think I can't see the dopey way you two look at each other?" Kate offered a lopsided smile as she stepped toward Naomi. "I don't want you to live your life around me, sis. The counselor said I have to focus on my future. You should too."

Sawyer knew Kate had been seeing the counselor almost daily for the past week. The sessions seemed to be helping, but he knew there was still a long way to go.

Naomi took Kate in her arms and hugged her. "Thanks, Kate. No matter what happens, though, I plan to stick with you through this."

"I know." Kate tentatively drew Sawyer into a three-way embrace. "And the best news of all is that I finally have the big brother I've always wanted."

Sawyer hugged them both.

If this was God's ultimate plan, he heartily approved.

READY TO READ Darby and Gage's story? Click here!

DEAR READER

I hope you are enjoying my Smoky Mountain Secrets series! You will get to meet all the foster kids in the rest of the stories. *Darby's Decision* is the next book, followed by *Cooper's Choice, Trent's Trust,* and *Jayme's Journey.* The entire series will be available this year.

Reviews are very important to authors, so if you enjoyed *Sawyer's Secret,* please consider leaving a review on the platform where you purchased the book. I would appreciate that very much!

I adore hearing from my readers! I can be reached through my website https://www.laurascottbooks.com/, through Facebook at https://www.facebook.com/ LauraScottBooks, Twitter at https://twitter.com/ laurascottbooks, and Instagram at https://www.instagram. com/laurascottbooks/. If you would like to hear about my latest releases, please consider signing up for my newsletter. I offer a free Crystal Lake novella to all who sign up. This book is not available for sale on any platform.

Until next time,

Laura Scott

PS. If you'd like a sneak peek at *Darby's Decision*, the first chapter is included for you here.

DARBY'S DECISION

Six years sober.

Darby Walsh took a moment to let that sink in, before kissing her five-year-old son, Leo, on the top of his head. "See you later, kiddo. Be good for Oma."

"I will." Leo slid a sideways glance at Edith Schroeder, the woman who had not only supported Darby during her stay at the halfway house after she'd finished rehab but had continued to provide a loving home for both Darby and Leo.

Darby wouldn't be alive and living with Leo in Knoxville today if not for Edith's support. She looked at the woman she loved like a mother. "I'm working the zip line today, so if you call and I can't answer right away, you'll know why."

"Not a problem. Leo and I are going to the park after breakfast." Edith smiled down at the rambunctious towhead. "We'll be fine."

"Great. See you both later." Darby left the side-by-side townhouse and headed to the Great Outdoor Adventure Park where she worked as a guide. She was proud of her sobriety and normally didn't dwell on the multitude of mistakes she'd made in the past.

But lately, she'd been thinking about her foster siblings, especially Hailey. For so long her focus was centered on providing a stable life for herself and Leo. Now she was becoming distracted by thoughts of reconnecting with Hailey and the other foster kids. Sawyer, Trent, Jayme, Caitlyn, and Cooper.

Oh, how she'd crushed on Cooper.

Darby arrived at the park and quickly headed inside the main building. The weather was warm and humid for mid-June, but their schedules were jam-packed thanks to the summer tourists.

"Hey, Darby," Teddy greeted her. Teddy was young, barely twenty-one, and followed her around like a puppy. She'd tried to let him down gently, she had no time or interest in a relationship, especially not with Teddy, but he'd continued to work his schedule to be paired up with her. "I'm working the zip lines with you today."

She suppressed a sigh. Of course he was. "Great. Let's check the gear and set up."

The park had seven different zip lines set at various heights and lengths. Darby loved zip-lining, the freedom of flying. Yet she took safety measures seriously, especially since she had Leo to consider. After methodically checking the cables, straps, and vests, she was satisfied they were good to go.

The first tour came up fifteen minutes later. A family of five, two adults and three teenagers.

Darby gave her usual lecture reiterating the rules and stressing safety. As always, she would go across the zip line first to show the group how things worked, and so she could stay on the other platform to help bring them in. Teddy would remain here to assist in getting their guests suited up and to secure their straps with the buckle clasps before sending them across to her.

"The key is to pull this strap here to slow down when you reach the other side," Darby explained. "But don't worry, I'll be there to grab you."

She tightened the strap on her helmet and clipped her vest and straps to the cable. "See you on the other side!" She pushed off.

Halfway across the cable, she heard a popping sound. Then the cable fell away, and she was free-falling.

Fingers of panic locked around her throat. At some level she heard the screams from the guests behind her, but there wasn't a moment to waste on them. Seeing the canopy of a large tree beneath her, she hoped for the best as she landed on the leafy branches. Her momentum threatened to push her off on the other side, dropping into the valley below, but she somehow managed to grab onto a tree branch with both hands, hanging on with every ounce of strength she possessed. She was lying on her stomach, hoping that the tree branches beneath her would hold up under the pressure.

"DARBY!" Teddy screamed her name from the platform behind her. But her position was such that she didn't want to move. Could barely breathe for fear of falling the rest of the way to the ground.

"We're getting out of here," a woman shrieked. "This isn't safe!"

Darby couldn't reassure them, even if she wanted to. Never in her life had she experienced something like this. These cables were strong enough to hold up to 250 pounds, and she weighed in at 125. She'd worked this park for the past several years without an issue.

What on earth had happened?

Moving very carefully, she turned her head to look behind her. She was too far away to see what had happened to the cable anchored into the pole holding up the platform. Teddy had gotten the family of five down to the ground and was hopefully getting their manager to call the fire department to rescue her. Thankfully, the first zip line is the shortest and the lowest of them, or she knew she would have suffered severe injuries.

Still could if the tree branches beneath her gave way before she was rescued.

A flash of movement below caught her eye. A man moving through the trees. She frowned, a chill washing over her. Had the cable been tampered with on purpose?

No, she was letting her imagination run away with her.

Wasn't she?

The park was full of tourists. *Get a grip*, Darby, she silently admonished. There was no reason for anyone to hurt her. Maybe in the past, in the days when she was associated with drugs, but not anymore.

The sound of a cracking tree branch made her freeze. How long would it take the fire department to get here? She tried to peer through the dense leaves to get an estimate of where the larger branches were. She'd hiked the wooden trails more times than she could count, but she hadn't spent much time climbing trees.

Not even as a kid. Living with the Preacher, a horrible evil man who'd physically and verbally abused her and her foster siblings, had not included fun activities like tree climbing. Quite the opposite. They'd knelt for hours on end listening to the Preacher yell and scream at them for being sinners, warning of God's fury. They'd slept in the cellar and were only allowed to do household chores and homework from Ruth, the Preacher's wife, who'd homeschooled them.

Another branch gave way beneath her, and she tightened her grip on the branch that had broken her fall. No point in thinking about the past now. She needed to be rescued and quickly. Leo needed her.

And she needed him.

"Hang in there, Darby," Teddy called. "They're coming soon."

"I'm doing my best. What happened?"

"It looks like there is damage in the pole around the spot where the cable was bolted in," Teddy said.

Damage? Like someone tampered with it on purpose? "How did we miss that?"

"I think the damage was camouflaged in some way." Teddy's voice sounded muffled now as if he was facing the opposite way. "Kent is pretty upset."

Kent Jacobs was their boss and the manager of the Great Outdoor Adventure Park. He was a decent guy, although he generally focused on making a profit. She knew he was likely more upset about losing the revenue from the zip lining than her fall.

The next hour seemed to go by in the blink of an eye. The firetruck arrived, and a fireman emerged in her line of vision. He stood in a large bucket that was within arm's reach.

"Ma'am? I need you to take my hand."

"I'm not sure I can do that," she confessed. Normally, she wasn't afraid of heights, but the thought of crashing to the valley below made her feel sick to her stomach. She was cold and sweating at the same time.

"I'm right here." The fireman's eyes were kind as he leaned toward her. "I don't want to put any pressure on the tree branches holding you up, so I need you to take my hand."

She didn't want him to put any pressure on the tree branches holding her up either. The fireman's outstretched hand was well within reach. Darby forced her fingers to let go of the branch to grab him.

When his fingers locked strongly around hers, she nearly wept with relief. From there, she was able to let go and take his other hand, allowing him to pull her toward him. Some of the branches gave way, but suddenly she was up and inside the bucket with the firefighter.

Safe.

Darby managed to thank him as they were lowered to the ground. The kind fireman helped her out of the bucket, and for a moment, her knees threatened to buckle.

"The ambulance is this way." The fireman put a hand beneath her elbow, intending to escort her to where the EMTs waited.

She instinctively dug in her heels. "I'm fine, just bruised and sore." Her entire body ached, but she ignored it. Frankly, going through withdrawal six years ago had been far worse than this. "No broken bones, see?" She held out her arms and waved them up and down.

"They'll need to check you over anyway," the fireman insisted. "You can refuse to go to the hospital by signing a waiver."

A waiver, much like the one their guests signed to participate in zip lining. The irony was not lost on her. Darby removed her helmet and headed over to the EMTs. She endured their exam, then signed the waiver indicating she chose not to be transported to the hospital.

"Darby, what happened up there?" Kent demanded.

She handed him the helmet and the rest of her gear. "I

was going to ask you the same thing. Teddy thinks the zip line cable was tampered with."

Kent flushed with anger. "Who would do something crazy like that?"

"I don't know, Kent. Certainly not me. Maybe you should have the experts come and examine it to find out what happened?"

Kent paled. "You think I need to call the police?"

"I think this needs to be investigated, yes. By the police and the experts." She glanced down at her scratched and bleeding arms and legs. Thankfully, her injuries weren't severe. "If you don't mind, I need to clean up." She moved to brush past him, but he lifted a hand to stop her.

"I'm glad you're okay. Take the day off, Darby." His voice was softer now. "We'll get to the bottom of what happened here."

She nodded and walked past him. The zip lines would be closed for the rest of the day, and maybe even the rest of the week. Today was Monday, how long would it take to repair the cable? Or would they simply close that particular zip line down?

Darby hated to admit it, but she wasn't keen on the thought of going back up.

As she walked back to her car, she saw a tall muscular man with dark hair standing there. Her steps slowed as she recognized him.

Gage Killian.

No, it couldn't be. Not after all this time.

A shiver of apprehension snaked down her spine. What was Gage doing here? She hadn't seen him since she'd betrayed him, giving his name to the police in exchange for a stint in rehab rather than being sent to jail.

A decision that still haunted her all these years later.

"Darby." Gage didn't smile, his green eyes serious. "I saw what happened. Are you all right?"

"You saw?" She remembered the figure she'd glimpsed walking down below and felt a rush of anger. "Did you tamper with the cable as a way to get back at me?"

"No."

She folded her arms over her chest, lifting her chin and meeting his gaze head-on. "I don't believe you. It can't be a coincidence that you show up here to find me at the same time a cable breaks away, sending me crashing into a tree. I can hardly believe I'm walking away from that with just scratches and bruises to show for it."

"I did not tamper with the cable," he said firmly. "But I would like to talk to you. If you have time."

Time? She choked and swallowed a hysterical laugh. No way was she making time for Gage Killian.

The last thing she wanted was for Gage to discover he had a son.

WATCHING Darby swinging through the air as the cable gave way had shaved ten years off Gage's life. His palms were still damp with sweat from fear. It was easy to understand her suspicion, his timing couldn't have been worse.

Or maybe it was perfect timing. While she was being rescued, he'd hovered near the firetruck, melting in with the other adventure park visitors, and had heard a young kid mention the cable must have been tampered with.

He'd gone hot and cold in a nanosecond.

Had Tyrone Reyes beat him here?

"Please move away from my car." Darby stared at him as if he had a third eye. "I have to go."

"Thirty minutes." These days, he wasn't much of a conversationalist. Being locked up in jail for four years, he'd kept to himself as much as possible. Attending Bible study sessions had become his salvation, but even then he hadn't done much talking, spending most of his time listening and soaking up the knowledge.

It had been strange how much talking he'd been forced to do since being released. He took a half step toward her. "Please."

Darby looked away, and he could tell she wasn't the least bit interested in talking to him.

"It's important," he urged. "I think I know who tampered with that cable."

She spun back to face him, her gray eyes wide. She wore her straight blonde hair shorter now, chin length rather than down to the middle of her back. The shorter length suited her. She looked beautiful and healthy. He was extremely relieved there was no sign of her being a drug user.

"Thirty minutes," she reluctantly agreed. "There's a coffee shop down the road. We'll walk."

"Okay." He was hardly in a position to argue. Darby gave him a wide berth, as if the idea of touching him, even in passing, was abhorrent. She headed down the blacktop driveway to the Keystone Coffee Café.

"How and why did you find me?"

Darby's abrupt question caught him off guard. He didn't want to come across as some sort of stalker, but then again, he'd called in a few favors to find her. "It's a long story."

She let out a snort, calling him on his lie. Well, not a lie exactly, but a half truth. This wasn't the time to get into all of that now, though. She'd only agreed to thirty minutes, and walking to the coffee shop had taken up a few of them.

They entered the coffee shop and found a table near the window.

"Do you still take cream and sugar?" He gestured to the cashier. "I'm buying."

"Yes." She didn't thank him, and she still looked as if she might jump up and run the moment his back was turned.

He hoped and prayed she wouldn't.

After buying two coffees, he returned to the table. Darby took hers hesitantly as if he might have poisoned it. The way she'd accused him of breaking her cable stung. She clearly didn't trust him in any way, shape, or form.

"Why are you here?" Darby didn't beat around the bush. She took a sip of her doctored coffee, eyeing him over the rim.

He decided to get straight to the point. "Tyrone Reyes is out of jail."

Her hand jerked, spilling some of her coffee. "Recently?"

"Within the past thirty days. You know as well as I do he's the type to seek revenge."

She stared down at her cup for a long moment before looking up at him. "He knows—everything?"

Gage knew what she was really asking. "He knows you gave me up to the police, and through me, got to him. So yeah, he knows everything."

Darby drew in a deep breath, then said very quietly, "I did what I had to do."

"I know." He couldn't lie and say it hadn't hurt. Yet at the same time, he'd understood she'd been forced to look out for herself. Honestly, wasn't that the reason he'd rolled on Reyes? It was the way the legal system worked. Small-time drug dealers like him were only snagged to get to the bigger fish. There was no such thing as honor among thieves.

Gage wasn't proud of what he'd done. He'd escaped one abusive situation only to find himself in a worse position. He'd admit he made poor choices and lived to regret them. He still thought of those months as the dark years, and he was determined to never, ever go back. But the months he'd spent with Darby wasn't all bad. In fact, she was the one and only bright spot in his mind.

Too bad she didn't feel the same way about him.

"You really think Reyes damaged the zip line cable in an attempt to hurt me?"

Darby's question pulled him from his thoughts. "I don't know. I didn't see him anywhere nearby, but he might have hired someone to do the dirty work for him. You're the one who mentioned the strange coincidence."

She lifted her gray eyes to his, and he saw a hint of defiance intermixed with fear. "Give me one good reason why I should believe you? You could have damaged the cable yourself, only to pin the deed on Tyrone Reyes." She hesitated, then added, "And you have a reason to get back at me, more than he does."

"I would never hurt you, Darby. And I don't blame you for what happened."

Darby let out a harsh laugh. "Yeah, right. How many years of jail time did you do because of me? Three?"

Four, with two years probation, but who was counting? "I mean it." He leaned forward, trying to get her to understand. "I don't blame you for ratting me out. It's each man or woman for themselves at a time like that. Besides, who do you think rolled on Reyes?"

She looked away. "I did. Although all I really knew was his name and that he pretty much made the drug deals that you carried out on his behalf."

"Yeah, well after they arrested me, I blabbed about

everything. I gave them details about Reyes and each of the drug dealers working for him, and lots of other information you couldn't possibly have known, Darby. And it worked, Reyes was busted right after me. In fact, I'm not sure how he managed to get out of the joint with a sentence of only five and a half years, unless he turned around and made the same deal."

Her gray eyes widened, and her voice dropped to a whisper. "You think Reyes turned on someone higher up in the organization?"

"Yeah, I do. But being forced to do that probably only made Reyes even more angry. The entire network had to have fallen to pieces by the series of arrests." Something he didn't feel the least bit sorry about. He hadn't gotten addicted to the stuff the way Darby had, but he'd stayed sober since being set free. And he had no intention of being involved in anything criminal ever again. "I firmly believe Reyes will come after me. In fact, I think he was responsible for my car being run off the road this past weekend." He'd suspected it wasn't an accident, but after watching Darby crash into a tree, he knew for sure it wasn't.

A flash of concern darkened her gaze. "You weren't hurt?"

"I'm fine." He waved a hand. "But if Reyes is responsible for the cable malfunction, he's definitely upped his game. The car collision wasn't nearly as serious as what you just experienced. I'm worried he'll keep trying until he's succeeded in hurting us, or worse."

Darby abruptly jumped up from her seat. "I have to go."

"Wait, shouldn't we . . ." but he was talking to the air as Darby had already bolted from the coffee shop, the door slamming shut with a loud bang behind her.

Made in the USA
Columbia, SC
12 April 2024

34303789R00134